JILL'S BIGGEST FAN

"What are you doing here?" Jill demanded, shocked to see Ryan at the rink.

"Aren't you going to say hi?" he asked. "After all, I did get up really early just so I could see you skate."

"You did?" Jill smiled.

Ryan nodded. "I don't really know much about figure skating, but you looked good. Really good. You must be the best skater here."

"Well, I am the only one in Silver Blades who goes to the International Ice Academy, so I guess you're right."

Suddenly Jill was aware of someone skating up to her. She turned and saw Kathy Bart stop right beside her. "What's going on here?" Kathy asked.

"A friend came to watch me skate," Jill said quickly.

"Then let's skate!" Kathy said. "Get going!"

Jill cringed. It was so embarrassing being treated like a baby by Kathy, especially in front of Ryan.

"I'll wait for you," he said. "We can catch some breakfast together when you're finished."

Jill watched Kathy skating away. Then she glanced at the clock on the wall and saw that she still had quite a bit of ice time left. Quickly she made up her mind. "You don't need to wait," she told Ryan. "I don't take lessons here anymore. And besides, I'm on vacation. Let's go now!"

Silver Blades

titles in Large-Print Editions:

SPRING BREAK

Melissa Lowell

Created by Parachute Press

Gareth Stevens Publishing
MILWAUKEE

For a free color catalog describing Gareth Stevens' list of high-quality books and multimedia programs, call 1-800-542-2595 (USA) or 1-800-461-9120 (Canada). Gareth Stevens Publishing's Fax: (414) 225-0377. See our catalog, too, on the World Wide Web: http://gsinc.com

Library of Congress Cataloging-in-Publication Data

Lowell, Melissa.
   Spring break / Melissa Lowell.
     p. cm. — (Silver blades; #9)
   Summary: When Jill returns to Seneca Falls on a vacation from the prestigious ice academy where she has been studying, her friends from the Silver Blades seem hopelessly immature, especially when she meets an older boy whom she wants to impress.
   ISBN 0-8368-2098-3 (lib. bdg.)
   [1. Ice skating—Fiction. 2. Conduct of life—Fiction. 3. Friendship—Fiction.] I. Title. II. Series: Lowell, Melissa. Silver blades; #9.
PZ7.L96456Sp 1998
[Fic]—dc21   97-40823

First published in this edition in 1998 by
Gareth Stevens Publishing
1555 North RiverCenter Drive, Suite 201
Milwaukee, WI 53212 USA

Printed in the United States of America

1 2 3 4 5 6 7 8 9 02 01 00 99 98

"**I**t's spring break!" Jill Wong cheered, hoping to get Bronya Comaneau's attention. But Bronya, Jill's roommate at the International Ice Academy, didn't even look up. She continued to sit silently at her desk on the other side of the girls' room, hunched over her history book.

How can anybody study at a time like this? Jill wondered. I've been skating and studying so hard for months. Now it's time to have some fun!

Giving up on Bronya, Jill glanced down at the rainbow of skating tights in her dresser drawer. She grabbed two pairs of red tights—her favorite color—and two pairs of black. Then she shrugged, scooped up the rest of her tights, and dumped them into her suitcase. She decided she'd take them all home to Seneca Hills with her. Everyone in Silver Blades will be dying to see me skate, Jill told herself. I have to look good every time I'm on the ice.

Silver Blades was one of the best competitive figure skating clubs in the United States, and Jill had been a member from the time she was eight years old. Since she'd been away at the Ice Academy, she missed her friends in the club—Danielle Panati, Tori Carsen, Nikki Simon, and Haley Arthur. They were all really serious about competitive skating, but Jill was the best skater of the bunch. She couldn't believe it when she'd been chosen to join the prestigious International Ice Academy in Denver, Colorado, last year. It had been hard to leave all her friends, but she couldn't pass up the chance to attend the Academy. And now she was going home where she could show her friends all that she'd learned on the ice.

Tossing her long black braid behind her back with a flick of her head, Jill carried several skating outfits over to her suitcase, rolling them up before she put them inside so they wouldn't wrinkle. Then she frowned. Jill wasn't going to spend all her time at home skating. She had to pack other clothes too. I want to look cool both on and off the ice, she told herself as she headed for the closet she shared with Bronya.

"I can hardly believe it. Two whole weeks of vacation," Jill said to her roommate. "I can't wear the same clothes every day." But Bronya kept reading and didn't comment. Jill sighed. Sometimes, like now, it was hard to get her attention. Jill didn't think she'd ever known anyone as serious about skating—or about studying—

as Bronya. At fourteen, Bronya was just a year older than Jill, but she'd already been at the Academy three years. And Bronya had come all the way from Romania to train here. My friends in Seneca Hills are serious, Jill thought, but not *that* serious.

Jill began riffling through her clothes, more determined than ever to take home just the right outfits.

"How about this?" Jill asked, trying again to draw Bronya into the excitement she felt. Poking her head and an arm out of the closet, Jill waved a black-and-red-plaid jumper at her roommate. "Should I take this, Bronya? Or do you think it looks too hot for spring?"

Bronya finally glanced up. "You'll have to decide," she said. "I don't know anything about the weather in Pennsylvania."

"You're right," Jill said, but she was pleased that she'd finally gotten Bronya to quit reading for a minute. "The weather is different there than it is here. It's wetter, for one thing. 'Damp,' as my mother likes to say. And the sun doesn't feel nearly as warm." Jill looked at the jumper again. "I guess I'll take it. No one at home has seen me in this, so they'll think it's new."

As Jill put the jumper into her suitcase, she glanced over at Bronya. "I'm going to miss you, Bronya," she said. Then she laughed. "But I bet you won't miss me. You'll finally get some peace and quiet once I'm gone." When Jill had first met Bronya, she hadn't thought her roommate was very friendly. But Bronya was just quiet, and after a while the two girls had gotten used to each other and had become good friends.

Bronya looked up again and smiled. "Of course I'll miss you, Jill. But you'll probably be too busy to miss me."

Jill laughed. "I'm going to have as much fun as I can while I'm home. I feel like I really need a break," she admitted. "Still, I wish you were coming with me. Or at least doing something fun. Anything but staying here."

"I don't mind. I'll skate a lot," Bronya said thoughtfully. "I don't want to lose the height I've worked so hard to get on my jumps. If I went to Seneca Hills with you, I'd just be in your way."

"No, you wouldn't!" Jill insisted. "All my friends would love you. They'd be so impressed by your skating. I'd show you the mall and—"

"But I want to stay here," Bronya said, cutting Jill off. "I like this place. It's more like home to me now than my home in Romania. Just look at it!" Bronya nodded at the girls' window. Through it, Jill could see the snowcapped Rocky Mountains. They are beautiful, Jill told herself. But it's beautiful in Pennsylvania too.

"I love the mountains here, and the rink is one of the best in the world," Bronya said. "Besides, I'm not the only one staying. There'll be things to do. I think we're going into Denver for a movie tonight."

"That's good," Jill said. "Everyone needs to take a break sometimes." Jill wasn't sure if her coach, Holly Abbott, would agree with that statement. She'd warned Jill to keep up with her practice schedule while she was away. Jill had promised her coach she would, but secretly she thought Holly would never know how much—or how little—practice time she really got in in just two weeks.

"You'll practice skating while you're home, right?" Bronya asked as if she could read Jill's mind.

"Oh, of course," Jill said. "All my really good friends back in Seneca Hills are competitive skaters. We'll all be hanging out at the rink."

Bronya smiled. "You've told me so much about Tori and Nikki and Danielle that I feel like I've already met them all. Let's see, Tori Carsen is the really competitive one whose mother designs clothes. Nikki Simon is a pairs skater, and her mom is about to have a baby. And Danielle Panati is your best friend. You call her Dani. She thinks she's too heavy so she's always trying to diet. Right?"

"Right," Jill said. "And then there's Haley Arthur. She's sort of new to our group. She has red hair and loves to fool around. But she's a great pairs skater. I wish you could meet them. I know you'd really get along."

"Maybe someday," Bronya said. "But not this vacation." She went back to her reading.

Jill continued traveling back and forth from her closet to her suitcase. When she returned with two pairs of jeans, she realized that her suitcase was bulging. I've just got to fit these jeans in, she thought.

She folded the jeans and put them on top of the pile of clothes. Then she tried to close the suitcase. No luck. Jill pulled and tugged. She tried rearranging things.

Finally, she sat on the suitcase and, with a few grunts, was able to fasten the clasps.

"There," Jill said, feeling relieved that she hadn't had to leave anything behind. "I think I've got everything." She crossed the room to her dresser and double-checked that her plane tickets were in her backpack. She felt a flutter in her stomach as she checked her watch. Her ride to the airport would be there any minute.

Glancing up at the mirror over her dresser, she checked her hair. She pulled a red ribbon from her top drawer and tied it onto the bottom of her braid. Then she adjusted her bow until it looked just the way she wanted it to. There would be a big crowd at the airport to meet her when she got off the plane, Jill was sure of it. And she wanted to look really cool for them all.

Suddenly there was a loud knock and a voice said, "It's Lisa Welch."

"Coming," Jill called back to Lisa, the dorm parent at Aspen House, the girls' dorm at the International Ice Academy. Lisa was also an instructor at the Academy. But she taught the younger skaters, so Jill had never worked with her.

"Your car service to the airport is here," Lisa said after Jill opened the door.

"I'm all set," Jill told her. "I'll be right down."

Lisa smiled. "Have a great time."

"I will," Jill assured her. She gave Lisa a hug.

After Lisa left, Jill turned back to Bronya. "Well, I

guess this is it," she said, feeling a twinge of sadness to be leaving.

"Good-bye, Jill," Bronya said, standing up and holding out her arms for a hug. "I'll see you soon. I want to hear tons of fun stories too."

Jill returned Bronya's hug. "Don't worry," she said. "I'll tell you everything." Then she slipped on her backpack and picked up her suitcase and skating bag. "This is it!" she said excitedly. "I'm on my way home!"

As Jill watched her plane climb above the clouds, leaving the Rocky Mountains far below, she recalled how excited she'd been to see those mountains when she'd first come to Denver. Now she was just as excited to be going home. As soon as this plane lands, she told herself, I'll be seeing Dani and Nikki and Tori and Haley and my mom and dad and my little brothers and sisters . . . everyone! She could hardly wait.

She dug her backpack out from under the seat in front of her and unzipped it. Then she pulled out her latest letter from Danielle Panati. Danielle had been Jill's best friend since third grade. Wait till Danielle sees how much my skating's improved, Jill thought as she unfolded her friend's letter.

"We all have the same two weeks off! Isn't that cool?" Danielle said in her letter. "Remember how Grandview Middle School and Kent Academy had different spring breaks last year? Nikki and I had to go to school while Tori and Haley got to skate all day. Then they had to go to school while we got to skate all the time. It'll be better this year. Now you and me and Nikki and Tori and Haley can hang out together for two whole weeks on and off the ice."

Jumping ahead to the end of Danielle's letter, Jill read, "We'll do everything we used to do in Seneca Hills. When we're through with that, we'll invent some new things. It'll be great!"

Jill folded Danielle's letter and put it away. But she kept thinking about her friends. She wondered if Tori would be as competitive with her as she sometimes was. Tori and Jill had always been in close competition with each other. But Jill was definitely the better skater, and sometimes Tori couldn't handle it. "I wonder what Tori will say when she sees my double axel," Jill murmured to herself.

Maybe Nikki's baby sister or brother would be born while Jill was home. Jill thought that would be great. She could help Nikki get used to the new baby. After all, Jill had six little brothers and sisters of her own, which gave her a lot of experience.

Jill wondered if Danielle would be into one of her crazy diets. Jill hoped she wouldn't be. When she wasn't dieting, Danielle was always up for a pizza or ice cream or some of Grandma Panati's baked goods. Just thinking about it made Jill feel hungry.

"Excuse me," the flight attendant said, interrupting Jill's thoughts. "What would you like to drink?"

"Cola," Jill replied, spotting the open can on the flight attendant's cart. At the Academy, fruit juice was always served. Ludmila Petrova and Simon Wells, the co-owners of the skating school, forbade soda and other junk food. Having a soda made Jill feel as if her vacation had finally started.

As soon as the plane landed, Jill straightened her bow and brushed off her oversize red cardigan and navy blue leggings. Satisfied that she looked good, Jill hurried off the plane. She was so excited she was grinning from ear to ear, and as she bounced down the walkway, it was all she could do to stop herself from running toward the waiting area. She was so eager to see everyone.

But as she hurried into the airport, what she saw stopped her short.

The only familiar face at the gate belonged to Mr. Wong, Jill's father. Jill hadn't been expecting banners or a school band, but she had thought her family and at least some of her friends from Silver Blades would be there. Jill's smile disappeared, and she dumped her backpack on the floor beside her. Where was everyone?

2

"**J**ill!" Mr. Wong cried, running over to his daughter.

"Dad!" Jill replied, throwing her arms around him. It was really great to see her father after all these months. He looked a bit heavier than he had last time Jill saw him. But otherwise he was still the slightly bald, stern-looking father Jill remembered. She gave him a big hug before asking, "Where is everyone?"

"Everyone?" repeated Mr. Wong. He seemed puzzled.

"You know," Jill said. "Mom and Henry and Kristi and the little kids." She looked around again, then added, "And my friends from Silver Blades. I thought that at least Danielle would be here to meet me."

"I don't know about Danielle," Mr. Wong said with a shrug. "But your mother had a few things to attend to. And your brothers and sisters decided to stay home with her." Mr. Wong smiled and shrugged again. "It is kind of a long car ride for everyone. And don't forget the time difference. It's later here than in Denver."

"I guess," Jill said, but she couldn't help being disappointed. Don't they care about me? she wondered. Aren't they glad I'm home?

She didn't want to complain, though. She wanted her father to see how much she'd grown up while she was away. Whining about her mother and friends not coming to meet her plane didn't seem very mature.

"Let's hurry to the baggage claim, Jill," Mr. Wong urged. "Your mother couldn't come to the airport, but she's eager to see you just the same. She gave me strict orders to rush you right home."

Oh, well, Jill told herself as she matched her father's quick pace toward the escalator. Maybe my friends forgot that I was coming home today. Or maybe they had something better to do, she thought with a pang.

Jill and her father rode the escalator to the lower level and found the baggage carousel that was unloading luggage from Jill's flight. Jill spotted her suitcase. Mr. Wong picked it up and led the way to the Wongs' green minivan. Jill followed, carrying her skating bag and backpack. When they reached the car, Mr. Wong set Jill's suitcase down as he unlocked the passenger door.

"Same old car," he said.

"Are you thinking of getting a new one?" Jill asked. They had bought the minivan right after the twins were born, when Jill was nine. Now she was thirteen and the twins were four. "We're about due for a new car," Jill said, noticing for the first time the rust spots around the door.

But Mr. Wong laughed. "Oh, no. No extra money for a new car, I'm afraid." He put Jill's suitcase in the back, then walked around the van and got in himself.

Jill and her father were silent as he found his way out of the maze of parking lots surrounding the airport. But once they were on the highway, Mr. Wong cleared his throat loudly. Jill might have been away from home for a few months, but she hadn't forgotten that her father's throat-clearing meant he had something important to say.

"What is it, Dad?" Jill asked. She was worried that he had something serious to talk about. Maybe it was about the family finances. Although Jill had a partial scholarship to the Ice Academy, the family had given up many things to pay for her lessons. Her mom had gone back to her job at the travel agency only a few months after Laurie was born. And she was always clipping coupons and searching for sales to save money.

Mr. Wong glanced over at Jill and laughed. "Don't look so grim, Jill. I've got good news."

"What?" Jill asked, feeling relieved.

"Your mother and I have arranged extra ice time for you," he said. "With Kathy Bart's help, of course."

"What do you mean? You called Kathy?" Jill asked, surprised to hear her father mention Kathy Bart, who had been Jill's coach at Silver Blades before Jill went to the Ice Academy. Kathy had once placed fourth in the Nationals and was an excellent skater and a very dedicated coach.

"Actually, your mother did the calling. Kathy says you can come to the rink and practice in the morning at the same time as your friends," Mr. Wong explained. "You can also skate from four to six in the afternoon. Isn't that great? Now we don't have to feel guilty for taking you away from the Academy for a couple of weeks. And you'll be able to stay in competitive shape right here in Seneca Hills."

"Thanks, Dad. That was nice of you," Jill said, staring out the window so her father couldn't see how she really felt. She hadn't planned on spending her vacation skating four or five hours every day. I need a little vacation from skating, Jill told herself. But how can I tell Dad that?

She knew her father put in overtime at his bank job whenever he got the chance. Jill didn't want to let him down after all he'd done for her. She decided not to say anything about her plans to get some rest. She also decided not to say anything about being a little mad that her parents had arranged the rink time without checking with her first. She was old enough to make her own plans. She didn't need her parents making calls for her.

"I do have a favor to ask you in return," Mr. Wong said as he turned off the highway.

"Sure, Dad. Of course," Jill said, bracing herself. She

knew she wouldn't be able to refuse her father's request no matter what it was.

"I'd like you to watch your brothers and sisters a couple of times while you're here," Mr. Wong said, stopping at a traffic light. "Your mother could use the break. Anyway, I'll let you know which days and nights we need you."

"No problem," Jill said, making her voice sound more cheerful than she felt. "I'd be happy to baby-sit."

"Only don't call it baby-sitting," Mr. Wong warned with a smile. The light turned green again, and Mr. Wong drove on. "Since he turned ten, Henry insists he's too old for a baby-sitter. Actually, he does a little sitting for us from time to time. But we don't like to leave him for too long or too late at night."

"I understand. And I'll be careful around Henry," Jill promised with a chuckle. She was looking forward to seeing her family again, but another part of her, a part she hated to admit even to herself, was a little resentful. Nearly all her days at the International Ice Academy were scheduled. When she did manage to get some free time, she often had trouble finding anyone to hang out with. She had been looking forward to having lots of freedom while she was at home and doing fun things with her friends. Only now, after talking with her father, it seemed as if she wasn't going to have much free time at all.

Jill knew she had a special duty as the oldest daughter in her family. She had to set an example for her younger brothers and sisters. But now, she told herself, after being at the Academy for a few months, it's going to be harder for me to be what Mom and Dad expect me to be. I've gotten used to being on my own, with only myself to think about in Colorado. This is going to take some getting used to. After all, I've grown up since I've been away.

"Well, here we are," Mr. Wong said as he turned down Browndale Avenue. The Wongs' house was the third one from the corner. It was a two-story white house with a red brick chimney and a green roof. A two-foot hedge lined both sides of their front yard. As they drove closer to the house, Jill saw that the hedge was just beginning to grow leaves again.

The sun was setting and the sky behind their house glowed a fiery red orange. Then she noticed that lights were on in the houses on either side of theirs. But there were no lights on at the Wongs'.

"Why is the house so dark?" Jill asked, feeling suddenly worried. With so many kids in the family, there were usually a lot of lights on.

But Mr. Wong didn't look particularly worried. "Maybe your mother had to go out for something," he said as he turned the car up the driveway.

"Without the minivan? Mom could never have fit everyone in the Toyota," Jill said, referring to the small tan car her father drove to work.

Mr. Wong still looked calm. "She could have taken the kids with her to the Minute Mart," he said.

Jill sighed. First her mother hadn't bothered to meet

her at the airport. And now she'd gone out. Some special homecoming this has turned out to be! she told herself glumly.

Mr. Wong parked the minivan in the driveway. After turning off the headlights, he started getting out.

"Aren't we going to park in the garage?" Jill asked. Her father always made a fuss about parking in the garage at night, because it was safer.

But Mr. Wong shook his head. "It'll be easier to bring these bags in the front door," he said as he pulled Jill's suitcase from the backseat. Jill gathered up her skating bag and backpack and followed him to the door.

"Let me get that for you," Mr. Wong said, reaching for the doorknob.

"That's okay—" Jill began to say.

But before she could finish, the front door burst open.

"Surprise!" a chorus of voices rang out.

3

"**I** don't believe it!" Jill gasped, dropping her things on the ground as the lights sprang on. Before her was a room full of familiar faces, all laughing and staring at her.

"Tori! Dani! Nikki! Haley! You're all here. You didn't forget about me after all!" Jill cried.

"How could we forget about you?" Tori asked, her blue eyes sparkling. She pushed a blond curl back from her forehead and chuckled. "You're all we've talked about for weeks!"

"You're all we've thought about for weeks too," Nikki added.

"Go on in, Jill," Mr. Wong urged from behind. "Don't just stand in the doorway! This suitcase is heavy."

Jill turned to her father. "Dad! You kept this a secret the whole time. I can't believe it!"

"Of course I did. It was a surprise. Now go on in," her father instructed. "The party's for you! Besides, I can smell your mother's cooking."

Jill inhaled deeply as she took a few steps into the house. "It smells delicious!" she said. "Just like the feast we always have for Chinese New Year!"

"Make room, everyone," Tori commanded as Jill's little brothers and sisters crowded forward. "Jill and your dad can't come in unless you guys back up some."

"How are you?" Danielle asked as she made her way to Jill's side. "I felt awful not going to meet you at the airport, but I didn't want to ruin the surprise." Danielle gazed at Jill anxiously with her big brown eyes. "You weren't too upset, were you?"

Jill hugged Danielle. "I was a little bummed. But I love this, Dani. Was it your idea?"

Before Danielle could answer, two pairs of little hands grabbed Jill's right and left hands. She felt herself being pulled farther into the house. Glancing down, she saw her four-year-old twin brothers, Michael and Mark.

"Look at the decorations, Jill," Mark said, tugging on her hand. "Me and Mike made them." Jill nodded and bent down to kiss her brothers.

"I love them," she said, taking in the red streamers draped across the living room ceiling. There were clusters of red and white balloons surrounding the entrance to the dining room, and a big banner with the words WELCOME HOME, JILL! on it.

"You guys do great work," Jill said, giving her brothers' hands an affectionate squeeze. "I love the drawings and stuff you've been sending to me at the Academy too. Your art is all over my room there. I look at it all the time. It really cheers me up whenever I feel homesick."

Mark's dark eyes suddenly looked worried. "Are you sick, Jill?"

"No, silly," Jill's eight-year-old sister, Kristi, answered for her. "She just means that she misses being home." Kristi hugged Jill and said, "You're going to be staying in my room with me, right?"

"Right. It'll be fun. Just like our own private slumber party," Jill told her; then she hugged her sister again. Kristi's room had been Jill's room until Jill left home.

Danielle reappeared with a Polaroid camera. "Hold it, you two," she ordered. Jill put her arm around her sister and smiled broadly. Danielle snapped their picture. "It'll be ready in a few seconds."

"How about one of me and Jill?" Tori asked. She patted her blond curls as she took Kristi's place beside Jill. "How do I look?" she asked.

"Great, as always," Jill said. "We don't call you the fashion queen of Silver Blades for nothing," she added as she nudged Tori playfully with her elbow. Tori really stood out tonight in her bright blue skirt and matching cashmere sweater.

"Don't I get a hug?" Mrs. Wong asked, coming up just as Danielle's camera flashed. She held a pair of pot holders in her hand.

As Jill gave her mother a hug, Danielle snapped another picture.

"I'm so glad to be home!" Jill told her mother. She sniffed the air. "Is that your shrimp toast I smell?"

"It's still your favorite, isn't it?" Mrs. Wong asked.

Jill nodded. "It sure is! But I love everything you make, Mom. You're the best cook in the world."

"Jill!" Laurie, Jill's youngest sister, sang out as she toddled toward Jill through the crowd. She had just learned to walk two months before. Jill picked her up and gave her a squeeze.

"You've put on weight," Jill told the chubby one-year-old as she set her down again. "I can't believe you're even cuter than I remember."

Jill felt a tap on her shoulder and spun around to see her ten-year-old brother smiling shyly at her.

"Henry! You've grown," Jill declared, giving him a hug even though she knew he'd hate it, especially in front of so many people. Her brother was almost as tall as she was now. "What happened to your hair? Did you join the marines?" she teased.

Henry laughed. "Give me a break, Jill. This is how all the cool guys wear it."

Jill noticed he wore baggy knee-length shorts and a T-shirt with a rap group's picture on it. Henry was definitely growing up! She gave him a playful punch on the arm just as Danielle's camera flashed again.

"What about me?" demanded Jill's six-year-old sister, Randi.

"I didn't forget about you," Jill said, and she gave Randi a hug too. Then someone put on a CD and Jill's favorite music, hip-hop, filled the house.

"I feel like dancing!" Jill exclaimed happily.

"Before anyone dances, I want everyone to have something to eat while the food's still hot," Mrs. Wong said. "You lead the way, Jill."

"Sure, Mom," Jill said. Now that she thought about it, she was starved. She made her way eagerly through the crowd, encouraging everyone she talked with to follow her to the dining room for a plateful of Mrs. Wong's specialties. Alex Beekman, Martina Nemo, Kelly O'Reilly, and other members of Silver Blades followed Jill.

Arranged on the dining room table were dishes of sweet and sour pork and fried wontons, egg rolls, and Jill's personal favorite, shrimp toast, squares of deep-fried bread and shrimp. Jill picked up a plate and started loading it up with food.

"What a feast!" Nikki declared, tucking a wisp of her brown hair behind her ear.

"It looks great," Haley agreed, squeezing in between Jill and Nikki. "Hi, Jill," she said, giving her red hair a toss. "How's Katarina?"

Jill laughed. "Still up to your jokes," she said.

Haley loved to pull tricks on her friends, and once she had convinced Jill that Katarina Witt, the gold medal winner in the 1984 and 1988 winter Olympic Games, was in the locker room at the rink signing autographs. Katarina was Jill's favorite skater, and Jill had fallen for Haley's little prank.

"That was one of my best jokes, wasn't it?" Haley said.

"It was kind of hard to laugh about it at the time," Jill recalled. "But I guess it was pretty funny," she admitted.

"Hi, Jill!" Kathy Bart said from the other side of the table. "I've been following you around for the last half hour trying to say hello, but I keep missing you. You move too fast!"

"Sarge!" Jill exclaimed, hurrying around the table to give her former coach a big hug. Kathy was one of the toughest coaches around, tougher than an army sergeant, the girls in Silver Blades often joked. But they never called Kathy Sarge to her face.

"Oops," Jill said sheepishly as soon as she realized her mistake. "Sorry, Kathy. It just sort of slipped out."

Kathy laughed. "Don't worry about it, Jill. I know everyone calls me that behind my back."

"You do?" Haley said, reaching for an egg roll.

"Yes. But please don't make a habit of it, okay?" Kathy gave Haley a stern look.

"Sure, Sarge. I mean, Kathy," Haley said, laughing.

Kathy pretended to scowl before turning to Jill. "Did your parents tell you yet that I've arranged for you to have lots of ice time while you're home?" Kathy picked up a fried wonton and dipped it in the red sweet sauce.

Jill nodded. She didn't want Kathy to see that she was less than thrilled by the idea, so she forced a smile. Jill planned on using the ice time that had been arranged for her, but she wasn't going to work really hard. Instead, she planned to have fun on the ice. Kathy doesn't need to know, though, she decided.

"Good," Kathy said. "Now I hope you've got lots of pictures of the International Ice Academy with you. I've looked at brochures of the place and I want to see what it's really like."

"I've got tons of great pictures," Jill assured her. "I could get them now if you want."

"Would you? I'd love it!" Kathy exclaimed.

Leaving her half-filled plate on the Wongs' dining room table, Jill ran to her backpack and dug out the pictures. The Ice Academy really is beautiful, she told herself wistfully as she flipped quickly through the photos.

Jill paused at a picture of Bronya in the middle of a perfect triple salchow. Bronya is so good! Jill told herself. Everyone at the Ice Academy is good—no, great! Jill knew a few of the students there would skate in the Olympics one day. Of course, the Silver Blades skaters dreamed of making it to the Olympics too. But the students at the International Ice Academy were that much closer to realizing their dreams. And I'm one of them, Jill thought. I'm one of those kids who's another step closer to the Olympics!

"Hurry up, Jill!" Tori yelled from the dining room.

"Coming!" Jill called. "Wait until you see these pictures!"

"What time should I pick you up after skating, Jill?" Mrs. Wong asked as she brought the minivan to a stop

in front of the Seneca Hills Ice Arena the following afternoon. "It's three forty-five now."

Jill shrugged. "I don't know." Kathy had told Jill to
take the morning off to unpack and spend time with
her family before she came to the rink. But now Jill
wanted to see who was around and catch up on all the
gossip.

"Quiet back there, kids," Mrs. Wong said. Everyone
except Henry had ridden along with Jill and her mother
that afternoon. Randi was arguing with the twins about
something, and Kristi was trying to teach Laurie to
count. At least that's what it sounded like to Jill. "What
did you say, honey?" Jill's mother asked.

"I said I don't know. I'd like to hang around for a
while after I skate," Jill said, speaking a little more
loudly.

Her mother shook her head. "You need to be more
definite. Should I pick you up at six-thirty, or could you
be ready sooner than that?"

Jill frowned. "Why do I have to say now?" she asked.
"Can't I just decide later and give you a call?"

"No. I have to plan when we're going to have dinner,"
Mrs. Wong said.

"Don't plan dinner for me, then. I'll eat a burger at
the snack bar or something," Jill said. She patted her
jacket pocket. "I have a little money." But she knew
she'd overstepped her bounds when her mother shot
her an angry look.

"I'm sorry, Mom," Jill said. "I'm not trying to be difficult." I just want to have fun, she thought. After all,
this is my vacation.

"Good. Then it's settled. I'll pick you up at a quarter past six. We'll eat at six-thirty," Mrs. Wong said firmly.

Jill knew there was no point in arguing. She opened the front door of the minivan and got out.

"Bye, everyone," she said before closing the door. Jill watched her mother drive away, then went inside.

The Arena looked the same as Jill remembered it. It was nice, but not as nice as the Academy's. In Denver the ice always looked as smooth as glass, and the lighting was mostly natural, from skylights in the ceiling that let in the bright sunshine. There were even trees planted around the rink, and flags from every country circled it. Somehow, the Seneca Hills Arena didn't look quite as impressive or professional.

Jill headed for the girls' locker room, wondering who she'd find inside.

"Jill!" Danielle called, waving to her from the bench near her locker, where she sat lacing up her skates. Danielle pulled off the silver headband that matched the short skating skirt she wore. After smoothing back her thick honey-brown hair, she replaced the headband and stood up.

"Cool outfit, Dani," Jill commented as she sat down and took her skates out of her bag.

"Thanks. I'll wait for you," Danielle said, sitting down on the bench next to Jill.

Jill put on her skates and started lacing them up. "That was a great party last night. Thanks, Dani."

Danielle smiled. "The food your mom fixed was fantastic. I loved seeing all your pictures too. It's just too bad it ended so early. We didn't even have much time to dance."

Jill nodded. "My parents don't like my little brothers and sisters staying up too late. Especially Laurie and the twins. They get really crabby when they're tired. And Dad did have to work today." Jill was also a little disappointed that her party had ended so early, but she had tried hard not to show it at the time. She knew that living at home again would take some adjustment.

"I think everyone understood," Danielle said. "All ready?"

"Ready." Jill smoothed the skirt of her red skating dress as she followed Danielle out of the locker room.

Once they got onto the ice, Kathy waved and skated over to them. "How do you feel today, Jill? Have you adjusted to this time zone yet?"

Jill nodded. "I feel great!"

"Good. I hope you brought your tape with you," Kathy said. "I want to see your new program. I've heard that you're landing your double axel all the time now. As I remember, you were just about to get it when you left for the Academy."

"It was the first thing I worked on with my new coach, Holly Abbott," Jill said. "Holly is an unbelievably tough coach, but it was worth it in the end."

"Come on, Jill, skate your program. I've been dying to see it," Danielle begged.

"Okay," Jill said. She couldn't wait to show Kathy and Danielle—and all the other Silver Blades skaters— how much she'd learned. "I'll get my tape. It's in my skating bag." Jill crossed the ice to the barrier. Slipping on her rubber guards, she hurried off the ice.

She returned with her tape a moment later and skated around the rink a few times to warm up. Then she headed for the booth where the tape player was located. Once her tape was in the player, she skated toward the center of the ice. She struck her opening pose and waited for the music to begin, conscious that not only Kathy and Danielle but several other members of Silver Blades as well were now watching her. She felt the familiar combination of tension and excitement she always experienced before performing. But this time it was even more intense. This time she had to show her audience how far she'd come. She had something to prove to herself, and to the Silver Blades skaters.

When the music started, Jill pushed off and began skating to the stately opening bars of Tchaikovsky's *Romeo and Juliet*, the music Ludmila Petrova herself had picked for Jill. Suddenly the music changed, becoming very fast, almost frantic. Here Jill did her complicated footwork sequence, building up the speed needed for her first jump, a triple salchow.

Everything was going perfectly until Jill came to her double axel. She began on the forward outside edge of her left skate. She kept her arms in and close to her body while she was in the air, just as Holly had coached her to. But when she landed, the edge of her blade seemed to hit a rough spot on the ice. Her ankle wobbled.

Oh, no! Jill thought. I'm going to fall!

4

Jill used her arms to steady herself and quickly regained her balance.

As she continued skating her program, she could almost hear her coach at the Academy yelling at her for spoiling her jump with awkward arm movements. Despite her disappointment, Jill gave the rest of her performance all her concentration. She quickly caught up with her music and finished her program with a dramatic layback spin.

"Bravo!" a chorus of voices rang out. Danielle and Kathy skated over. Several of the other Silver Blades skaters followed.

"That was terrific, Jill!" Kathy said, giving her a quick hug. "They're doing great things for you at the Academy. I can tell."

But Jill knew Kathy was wrong. She knew her performance hadn't been terrific at all.

"My double axel is really much better than that," Jill insisted, shaking her head. "The surface here isn't as well groomed as it is at the Academy. I hit a rough spot and it messed me up."

"The ice was just cleaned before you came out," Kathy told her in an even tone. Jill knew that Kathy was proud of both Silver Blades and the Arena where the club practiced. They were the center of Kathy's life.

"I know what I felt," Jill insisted, "and I felt a rough spot. At the Academy, the ice is incredibly smooth."

"I'm sure you're right," Kathy replied in a tight voice.

But Jill could tell that Kathy was just trying to be agreeable and that she really didn't think there was anything wrong with the ice. "It's just that I've gotten used to a perfect surface to skate on," Jill continued. "Not that there's anything wrong with the ice here. It's always been—"

Suddenly Kathy interrupted, saying, "Well, I've got to get back to work now. Everybody else better get moving too. Come on, Danielle. Let's start on those spins we talked about," she said as she skated away.

"I thought Mr. Weiler was your coach," Jill said to Danielle as she watched Kathy cross the ice.

"He is," Danielle said. "Kathy's working on a couple of spins with me, that's all."

"Be careful over in the far corner, Dani," Jill warned. "There's a rough patch that could throw you."

Danielle looked off to where Jill pointed. Then she

turned back to Jill. "This rink has never given any of us a problem," she said. "I don't get it."

"Well, maybe if you skated on the Academy's ice, you'd know what I mean," Jill said.

"Yeah, maybe," Danielle said, staring down at her skates. "Well, Kathy's waiting for me. I'd better go. Want to meet at the snack bar after practice?" Danielle asked.

"I do, but I can't," Jill said. "My mom's picking me up right afterward."

"Maybe tomorrow," Danielle said hopefully. Then she skated after Kathy.

Jill started circling the ice. I'm going to land my double axel again, she promised herself. And this time it's going to be perfect, no matter what the ice is like!

"But, Mom, I just got home for my break, and I want to hang out with my friends," Jill said to her mother as they pulled up in front of the rink early Tuesday morning.

"I know, honey, but I need you to baby-sit," Mrs. Wong said. "I promised Henry, Randi, and Kristi I'd buy them new shoes today, and I can't bring the little ones with me. You know how they are when you take them to a store."

Jill sighed loudly. "But you're planning all my time for me, Mom. First it was the practice time at the rink.

Now it's baby-sitting. My whole vacation is almost filled up with your plans instead of mine."

"I thought you'd want the time at the rink, Jill," Mrs. Wong said. "We did that as a favor to you. We thought you'd want to keep in top shape."

There was nothing Jill could say to that. She knew her mother was right. It just bugged her that she wasn't allowed to decide when she'd skate, and how often. And now her mother had decided what she'd do with her time between practices too.

"It's just that I had different ideas about what I'd do with this vacation," Jill said.

"And I want you to have a good time on your vacation too," Mrs. Wong said. "But I count on you to help out."

Jill didn't want to argue with her mother, not if she was going to be home for only two weeks. "Okay, okay. I'll baby-sit for you after morning practice," she said, climbing out of the car.

Jill shut the door just as her mother was telling her what time she'd pick her up. "See you later," Jill said without even looking back.

"I landed my double axel four times today!" Tori said excitedly. The Silver Blades extra-long holiday morning session had just ended, and the girls were changing in the locker room. "I can't wait to tell my mother about it. Mr. Weiler said I looked really good."

"I can see you've come a long way with it," Jill said as she took off her damp T-shirt. "But I don't think you really have the double axel down yet."

Jill had decided she would do Tori a favor by being honest with her. The more Jill thought about Kathy's comments on Jill's performance on Monday—after she almost fell when she landed her double axel—the more Jill realized that Kathy wasn't as tough a coach as she had always thought she was. Jill's new coach at the Academy would have been much more critical—and helpful. Even though Jill had found the criticism hard to take at first, she now realized that listening carefully to criticism was the only way to get better. Kathy was just too soft with me, Jill told herself, and so is Mr. Weiler with Tori. And I should try to help Tori if I can.

"Wait a minute," Tori said, glaring at Jill, her arms folded across her chest. "What exactly do you mean? What's the matter with my double axel? Mr. Weiler didn't seem to think there was anything wrong with it. In fact, he said, 'I think your double axel is coming along nicely, Tori.'" Tori did a perfect imitation of Mr. Weiler, and Nikki and Haley giggled.

"Well, your double axel probably is coming along nicely," Jill said, deciding to let the matter drop. Getting into a fight with Tori was the last thing she wanted.

But Tori persisted. "That's not what you just said. If you think I'm doing something wrong, I want to know what it is."

"Okay," Jill said. "You look like you're in pain when

you pull your arms and legs in. Your rotations look forced. Relax a little, Tori. You'll look more graceful if you do."

"So you think I look like a clod?" Tori demanded. Her blue eyes flashed angrily.

"I didn't say that," Jill replied.

"Of course you did. Didn't she, Haley?"

Haley looked at Jill apologetically and shrugged. "Not exactly, Tori."

"You asked Jill for advice, Tori," Danielle said. "If you don't agree with Jill, forget about it."

"Dani's right, Tori," Nikki agreed, zipping up her warm-up jacket. "It's only advice. It's up to you whether or not you want to follow it."

Jill's frown deepened. She was right about Tori's double axel, and she knew it. "If you had serious coaches like the ones I have—" Jill began.

But Tori cut her off. "Are you saying that Mr. Weiler isn't a good coach? I can hardly believe it! He's one of the best there is!"

"Well, maybe you think so," Jill said.

"Lighten up, guys," Danielle said, stepping between Tori and Jill but looking at Tori. "Jill's on vacation."

"So am I," Tori shot back.

"That's exactly why we shouldn't fight and spoil everything," Danielle said.

"Cool sweatshirt, Jill," Haley commented, changing the subject.

"And it's even your favorite color," Nikki added as she pulled on her light blue Silver Blades warm-ups over the gray leggings and oversize green T she'd just skated in. "Are the Ice Academy's colors red and silver, Jill?"

Jill shook her head. "The Ice Academy doesn't have colors. It's not a club like Silver Blades. It's a serious skating school. Anyway, they had this sweatshirt in a bunch of different colors. Naturally, I picked red."

"Naturally," said Tori.

"Hey, let's all go over to my house," Danielle said. "I'm sure my grandmother would be happy to fix us brunch."

"I can't," Jill said.

"Oh, come on, Jill," Tori said. "I'm willing to drop this whole thing if you are. Dani's right. I don't want to fight. Especially not with you."

Jill shook her head. "That's not it, Tori. I have to baby-sit for my mom now. She'll be here any minute to pick me up."

"Okay, then," Danielle said. "How about coming over later today? After our afternoon session? I promised that you'd have fun while you're here, Jill, and I always keep my promises."

"Sorry. I can't," Jill said, shaking her head again. "My afternoon ice time is after yours. I have to skate from four until six and you guys skate from twelve to two, right?"

"Why four to six?" Nikki asked.

"I don't really know exactly. My parents set up this schedule with Kathy," Jill explained.

"You don't sound too wild about it," Tori said.

"I'm not. At the Ice Academy I skate six hours a day

six days a week," Jill told them. Just thinking about her heavy schedule made her feel tired.

"Wow!" said Haley. "That's fantastic. I wish I got to skate that much all the time."

"Don't get me wrong," Jill said. "I'm not complaining about that—not exactly. It's just that these two weeks at home were supposed to be a break, you know? But my parents have a different idea. They want to make sure I stay in competitive shape. And they think that I should spend all my free time with them—or with my brothers and sisters. I know they've missed me, and I've missed them too. But there are other things I want to do."

"You sound pretty upset," Danielle observed.

Jill nodded. "I guess I am. I've been working so hard the last couple of months that I really need a little time off."

"Tell them how you feel!" Tori suggested. "Isn't that what you told me I should do with my mom, Jill? Remember? When she was trying to run my life?"

"She's right, Jill," Danielle said. "I know your parents pretty well and I'm sure they'll understand that you want to spend time with us off the rink too."

Jill shrugged. "I told my mother that this morning. But she told me she counts on me to help out. And I'm going to be home for only two weeks."

"I know what we can do," Danielle said. "We'll come up with a plan. Something really big that your mother can't say no to. We'll decide on something cool to do while we're having brunch at my house. Then we'll call you and let you know."

Jill smiled. Suddenly she felt better. "You guys are the greatest!"

"When will Mom be home?" Mark asked for the fourth time.

"In a while," Jill said with a sigh. Mrs. Wong had been gone only half an hour. She'd taken Henry, Randi, and Kristi to the mall and had left Jill at home with Laurie and the twins. I don't seem to be doing a very good job of entertaining them, Jill decided.

Then suddenly she had an idea. "Want to go to the park?" she asked, remembering that the twins had always loved going to the park, which was only a couple of blocks from their house.

"Oh, boy!" the twins shouted, jumping up and down.

"Park!" Laurie cried.

"All right then!" Jill said, pleased that her baby-sitting know-how was finally coming back. "Let's go!"

Once they were outside, Jill pulled the family's red wagon out of the garage. She helped Laurie into it and let the twins add a ball and a toy dump truck that they both loved. With Jill pulling the handle, they headed down the sidewalk toward the park.

They'd gone only a block when the boys decided they were too tired to walk anymore. Jill helped them into the wagon. Pulling was slow going now, and Jill was relieved when they finally reached the park.

"Everybody out!" she said.

"We want to slide!" the boys cried.

"Swing," Laurie said firmly. Jill laughed at the sound of her baby sister's determined voice. But then, Laurie had to be certain about what she wanted, Jill told herself, or she'd never get anything. Not with Michael and Mark around.

"Okay," Jill said. "You boys can slide. Laurie and I are going over to the swings."

Jill took Laurie's hand. But as they neared the swings, Laurie pulled her hand away and started running. Jill followed at a slower pace, until she saw something move in the bushes behind the swings. Quickly she hurried to catch up to her little sister, but it was too late. A huge dog sprang out of the bushes. He paused for a minute, sniffing the air. Then he spotted Laurie and let out a loud, deep bark.

Jill started to run. But before she could reach Laurie, the dog started running too. His mouth was open and his tongue dangled out over a terrifying set of teeth. The big dog was headed right for Laurie!

5

"**L**aurie!" Jill screamed, leaping forward. As she scooped her sister up in her arms, they both tumbled to the ground.

The big dog bounded up and stood over them, panting and drooling.

"Go away," Jill yelled at the dog sternly. She didn't think the dog looked dangerous anymore, but she couldn't be sure. "Go home," Jill ordered again. But the dog didn't move. If anything, Jill's words seemed to make him more excited. He barked again. Laurie started to cry and twisted in Jill's arms.

"It's all right, Laurie," Jill said, doing her best to sound calm. But Laurie kept on struggling. "He won't hurt you," Jill told her.

"Groucho!" Jill heard someone yell from somewhere on the other side of the bushes. Then a boy appeared.

He had shoulder-length brown hair and wore black jeans, a thick flannel shirt, and hiking boots. Jill saw he was holding a leash.

"What's wrong with you?" Jill demanded angrily as she sat up. "That dog shouldn't be off his leash. Seneca Hills has a law about letting dogs run free, you know, especially vicious dogs!"

As the boy bent over, his long hair fell forward, covering his face for a minute. He snapped the leash onto the dog's collar, then straightened up, raking his hair back into place with his hand. Jill couldn't believe it when he started to laugh.

"It's hardly funny," Jill snapped, growing angrier by the moment. She sat up straighter but kept a firm hold on Laurie. "That dog could have hurt my sister. You had no business taking him off his leash."

"This dog wouldn't hurt a fly. He wouldn't have attacked you," the boy said, still smiling. "He's really gentle. See?" He started petting the dog, which quickly collapsed in an obvious fit of pleasure.

"Well, we didn't know that," Jill said stubbornly. "He ran right for my sister. Even if he wasn't going to bite her, he could have knocked her down. She could have been hurt."

"Look. I'm sorry. Okay?" the boy said. "Groucho loves little kids so much, he gets overexcited sometimes when he sees one. I wouldn't have let him off the leash if I'd known you were there." The boy looked hopefully at Jill with his warm brown eyes.

"Doggie?" Laurie said, reaching her hand out in the dog's direction. Jill quickly pulled her arm back.

"She can pet him if she wants," the boy said. "Groucho won't hurt her. That's my dog's name—Groucho," he added.

"Well, okay," Jill said, letting go of her sister's arm. "You can pet him, Laurie." Laurie stood up and tentatively petted the dog's golden coat. Groucho wagged his tail.

"See?" the boy said, clearly pleased by what was happening.

"All right," Jill said. "You've proven your point. He likes little kids."

"I'm Ryan McKensey," the boy said. "And you're . . ."

"Jill Wong," Jill said as she stood up. When she was at his level she noticed for the first time how good-looking he was. His big brown eyes had a touch of gold in them. He was tall and thin and looked athletic. She brushed the leaves off her jeans and was suddenly conscious of how she was dressed. She wished she were wearing something nicer than her old jeans and a red sweatshirt.

Jill looked back at Ryan and decided he was even cuter than she'd first thought. She wasn't sure what to say next, so she introduced her little sister to him. "That's Laurie. She's one year old."

"Nice to meet you, Laurie. I hope you can forgive me and Groucho for scaring you."

Laurie looked up at Ryan. "Hi!" she said. Then she went back to petting the dog.

Jill was searching for something to say again. She didn't have a lot of experience with boys—except for her brothers and the boys who skated with Silver Blades or at the Ice Academy. But before she could come up with something, Michael and Mark ran up.

"These two are my little brothers," Jill explained.

"Twins?" Ryan said, and Jill nodded.

"What's his name?" Michael asked, pointing at the dog.

"Groucho. What's your name?" Ryan countered.

"I'm Mike, and that's Mark," Michael said.

"Can he play ball?" Mark asked, pointing at Groucho.

"Not with a leash on," Ryan answered. He looked at Jill and lifted his eyebrows as if he were asking for permission. Jill couldn't stop herself from smiling back. The dog did seem gentle enough. Jill didn't think he'd bite anyone. But he was still big. He could easily knock down not only Laurie, but Mark and Michael as well. Jill didn't know what to say.

Once again she was saved by one of the kids. Laurie tugged on her hand and said, "Swing. Swing."

"My sister wanted to swing," Jill said. "I promised she could, and we haven't yet."

"I'm a great swing pusher," Ryan bragged.

"Will you push us?" Michael asked eagerly.

"Maybe," Ryan said, still looking at Jill. "If it's all right with your big sister."

"Come on, Jill," Michael begged. "Please?"

Jill laughed. "Sure," she said, feeling herself relax a

little. "Push away if you want to. It'll be less work for me."

"Yahoo!" the twins cheered. They started running toward the swing set.

"Wait a minute. What'll I do with Groucho?" Ryan said, looking at Jill.

"Oh, all right," Jill finally relented. "Let him go."

"He'll stay if I tell him to," Ryan assured her. "Watch." Ryan unfastened Groucho's leash, then said, "Sit. Stay." Groucho sat and stared attentively at Ryan. When Ryan walked away, the dog stayed put.

"I took him to obedience school," Ryan explained. "He's a golden retriever. They're really smart dogs." Jill nodded. She knew less about dogs than she knew about boys. But Groucho seemed pretty nice now that she'd gotten to know him a little.

Mark and Michael each sat on a swing. Meanwhile, Jill helped Laurie into the baby swing and fastened the chain across the front.

"Who's first?" asked Ryan.

"Me! Me!" the boys cried out.

"Don't ever say, 'Who's first?' to twins," Jill advised Ryan in a teasing voice, glad that she was finally able to start a conversation. "Just decide yourself as quickly as you can. By the time the one who's second figures out what's happening, it's his turn anyway."

"Good advice," Ryan said. With that he took hold of Mark's swing and gave it a swift push.

"Now me!" pleaded Michael. "Me!"

After he'd given each boy several pushes, Ryan said, "Okay, that's it. Time to do something else now."

"Awww!" the boys complained. They looked at Jill, and she nodded.

"Want to play fetch with Groucho?" Ryan asked. Then he quickly turned toward Jill. "That is, if it's all right with Jill."

The twins hopped off their swings and dashed over to their sister. "Please, Jill," they begged.   .

"All right," Jill said, deciding that both Ryan and Groucho, who still sat where Ryan had left him, had more than proven themselves.

Mike took the ball out of the wagon and threw it a few feet away from the dog.

"Go on," Ryan told Groucho. "Get the ball." Groucho barked once, then went after the ball.

Jill laughed. "Your dog is pretty funny, isn't he?"

"Why do you think I named him after the funniest Marx brother?" Ryan answered.

Jill didn't want to admit that she didn't know who the Marx brothers were.

"Down," Laurie said just then. Jill unfastened the chain and helped Laurie to the ground. As soon as her feet hit the sand, Laurie toddled after Groucho and the boys. For a minute Jill worried that Groucho would notice Laurie and run at her again. But he was apparently having too much fun with the twins.

"So I guess you have to baby-sit a lot, huh?" Ryan asked, sitting down on one of the swings.

"Yeah. I have two more sisters and another brother

at home," Jill said, sitting on the swing next to Ryan's. "There are seven of us in all. Nine counting my mom and dad."

Ryan smiled as he rocked back and forth. "Wow! You're lucky. Big families are fun."

"Do you have any brothers or sisters?" Jill asked.

"I wish I did, but I don't. I'm an only child. Unless you count Groucho, that is." He laughed, and Jill realized he was nervous too. She smiled and felt herself relax a little.

"So," Ryan asked a moment later, "do you live around here?"

Jill nodded. Then she remembered that she didn't really live in Seneca Hills anymore. She lived in Denver. "Actually my family lives here," she said, "but I don't. How about you?"

"I live a block over that way," Ryan said, nodding toward the bushes Groucho had sprung out of. "We live on Sunnyside."

"We live on Browndale. It's a block that way." Jill nodded in the opposite direction. Then she giggled and added, "I mean, my family does."

"All right. Where do *you* live, then?" Ryan asked, looking at her as if he suspected she was setting him up for a joke. "And why don't you live with your family?"

"I live in Denver," replied Jill. "I'm a figure skater. I go to the International Ice Academy."

"Wow," Ryan said. He sounded impressed. "You must be really good."

Jill shrugged. "Good enough to be invited to go there. Where do you go to school?" she asked, to change the subject.

"Seneca Hills High," he said.

"Oh?" Jill wondered if he knew she was just a seventh-grader or if he thought she was older. "What grade?"

"Ninth," he said. "How about you?"

Thinking fast, Jill said, "I'm not in any grade anymore. I have a private tutor at the Ice Academy."

Ryan whistled. "That sounds pretty fancy."

Jill laughed. "It's not really. It's just that we skate so much, we don't have time to sit through a regular school day like the ones I had here at Grandview."

"Grandview," Ryan repeated, frowning. "Isn't that a middle school?"

Jill felt herself blush. Now what am I going to do? she wondered. Lie? But she couldn't bring herself to do that.

"I'm a seventh-grader," Jill admitted. "Or I was. I'm thirteen." When Ryan's eyebrows shot up, Jill said, "Is there something wrong with that?"

"No. Of course not. It's just that I thought you were older. You seem older." Ryan laughed. "What am I saying? I'm just a couple of years older than you are. Big deal, right?"

Jill smiled. "Right," she said. She tried to act casual, but really she was thrilled that he'd thought she was older than she was.

"In fact, until we moved here a couple of months ago, I was in junior high. Back in Wisconsin, where I used to live, we had junior high instead of middle school and junior high included ninth grade," Ryan explained.

"You're from Wisconsin?" Jill said.

Ryan nodded. "We moved because my dad got a job with MicroTech—you know, that big software company over in Burgess."

"Really?" Jill didn't know much about computers, but her brother Henry was interested in them. And, of course, her father used computers in his work at the bank. "Are you interested in computers too?"

Ryan shook his head. "They're all right. But I don't want to be a programmer like my dad. I want to be a veterinarian like my mom. When we lived in Wisconsin, she worked mostly with cows and cow diseases, though. I plan to specialize in big dogs. You know, like Groucho."

"Look!" Ryan said, pointing toward the slide. "Your little sister is on top of the slide! She's a good climber. How often—"

"Oh, no!" Jill cried when she realized what Ryan was saying. "She might fall!" Jill sprang off the swing and started to run.

She reached the slide in seconds and scrambled up the ladder after Laurie. When she got to the top, Jill sat down and put Laurie in her lap.

"Wow. You're fast," Ryan said to Jill.

Jill smiled down at him, then went down the slide with her sister.

"You know, guys, it's about time for us to go home," Jill announced. She put Laurie in the wagon. Mike and Mark climbed in after she called them over.

Suddenly Ryan was right beside her. He had the twins' ball in his hand, which he handed to Mark. "Will I see you around here again?" he asked Jill.

For a second Jill felt confused and didn't know what to say.

She was still trying to decide how to answer when Ryan said, "How about going out with me? Maybe Friday night?"

"A date?" Jill asked before she could stop herself.

Ryan laughed. "I guess that's what it's called. Yeah. A date."

Jill felt herself blush. "I don't know what to say," she admitted.

"Say yes, unless you've got something else to do."

"Okay," Jill said firmly, suddenly making up her mind.

"Okay. Good! I mean, great! I don't know what we'll do yet. Something. I'll look up your number in the phone book and I'll call you." Then he turned and took off at a run, Groucho at his side.

Jill couldn't believe it. She stood for a moment after he'd left, staring at the spot where he'd disappeared behind the bushes.

"A date," she whispered to herself. "A real date."

She turned and picked up the handle to the wagon

and started pulling it toward the sidewalk. After taking a few steps, she stopped. Suddenly a question had come to her mind, something she hadn't thought of when Ryan had asked her out.

"What am I going to tell my parents?" she wondered out loud.

6

"**W**e did it. We got you away from both the Ice Arena and your family," Danielle said as she slid into a booth at Super Sundaes on Wednesday afternoon.

"Finally," Jill added with a laugh.

"What did your mother say when you told her we were taking you out for a special Silver Blades lunch?" Haley asked as she sat down next to Jill.

"She said, 'Be sure to keep track of the time, Jill. You don't want to miss any of your afternoon practice,'" Jill said, imitating Mrs. Wong's no-nonsense voice. Nikki and Tori laughed as they slipped into the booth.

Tori shook her head. "I always thought your mother was pretty cool, Jill. Not like my mom. She has to keep her eyes glued on me every second—on or off the ice. And then she has to tell me everything I've done wrong."

"My mom's not like that," Jill said. "And she would *never* tell me how to skate. It's just that both Mom and Dad think I want to spend my time skating. And if I'm not on the ice, they want me to spend as much time with the family as possible. They're really happy to see me. But I want to do other stuff, like hang out with you guys."

"It sounds like there just isn't enough of you to go around, Jill," Nikki teased as she unzipped her lightweight spring jacket. She fixed her green eyes on the menu. "You know," she said, "everything looks so good."

"Everything *is* good," Danielle said. "But we're not going to have just anything. We're all going to have Super Sundaes' famous Make-Your-Own Sundaes," she declared, wiggling her dark eyebrows mischievously.

"I'm not sure I can afford that," Tori said, shaking her head.

"Don't worry," Danielle replied. "My grandmother gave me a twenty this morning. Yours is on me."

"I have money," Tori said. "I was talking about calories. And what about your diet, Dani?"

"Diet? What diet?" Danielle said cheerfully.

A waitress came to the table. After she left with their order for five Make-Your-Own Sundaes, Nikki turned to Jill.

"All right. Now tell us the exciting news you said you had. The news that you couldn't tell us in the locker room or on the bus," she said.

Ryan's face sprang into Jill's mind, and she smiled. "I'm not sure where to begin," she admitted. Should I start by telling them what he looks like? she wondered. Or should I start by telling them how nice he is?

"It must be something really good," Haley said, poking at the ice in her water glass with a straw. "Look at that big grin on Jill's face. Did you play a joke on someone?"

"You're the prankster, not me," Jill replied with a laugh.

"Okay, quit stalling, Jill," Tori demanded. "You know you can't keep anything from us. Now, what is it?"

"Actually, I met someone," Jill said. She felt her smile widen. "Someone really special and cool."

"A boy?" Nikki asked eagerly.

Jill nodded. Then everything Jill knew about Ryan came out in a rush. "He's new in town. His name is Ryan and he's fifteen. He goes to Seneca Hills High and has a dog named Groucho. He wants to be a vet. His eyes are brown. He's tall and his hair is sort of long and incredibly cool. He lives only a couple of blocks from me and—"

"Whoa! Wait a minute," Tori said, cutting Jill off. "Just how did you meet this cool guy?" she asked suspiciously. "I thought that ever since the welcome-home party you've either been skating or with your family."

Jill nodded. It was pretty amazing now that she thought about it. She never would have dreamed that she'd meet such a cute guy while baby-sitting. "I was at the park with Laurie and the twins when Ryan showed up. I thought his dog was going to attack us. But luckily I was wrong," she said.

"Attack you?" Nikki and Haley asked in unison.

"Groucho is a golden retriever," Jill explained, remembering how cute Ryan was with his dog. "They're very gentle dogs."

"Nobody cares about his dog, Jill," Tori said impatiently. "Tell us what happened next. You met Ryan and . . . ?"

". . . and he asked me out!" Jill shrieked excitedly.

"Really?" the other girls asked, leaning toward Jill, their eyes wide.

"How cool," Haley said dreamily. "A real date with a real high-school guy! You have all the luck, Jill."

"When are you going out?" Tori asked. "What are you going to do?"

"We're going out this Friday night," Jill said. "But I don't know where yet."

"Friday!" Tori said not at all happily. "But we were going to have a slumber party at my house on Friday night. That's the plan we came up with."

"Get real, Tori!" Danielle said.

"You're right, Dani," Tori admitted. "A slumber party isn't even half as cool as a date with a high-school guy."

"How about moving the slumber party to another night?" Nikki suggested. "Maybe Saturday? We've just got to."

"I'll have to ask my mom," Tori said. "I'll let you guys know."

"When do we get to meet this guy?" Nikki asked. "He sounds fantastic."

"He is," Jill agreed. "And he's not just cute. He's really nice too. And funny." And just a little bit shy, Jill added to herself, which makes him just about perfect!

"He's also older. What do your parents think? Do they want to meet him first?" Danielle asked.

Suddenly Jill frowned. She hadn't figured out yet what she was going to tell her parents.

"What's the matter, Jill?" Danielle asked. "Didn't you tell your parents?"

Jill shook her head. "Do you think I should?" she asked nervously.

"Don't you sort of have to?" Danielle pointed out.

"But what if they say no?" Jill asked. "I mean, I already said yes to Ryan!" Jill shook her head again. She'd feel like such a baby if her parents said no. "I can't risk it. I really want to go out with Ryan, and this may be my only chance. I'm leaving next week."

"I definitely agree with Jill," Tori said. "Telling her parents is way too risky. They might say she can't go out with Ryan. They might say he's too old for her or that she isn't allowed to date at all. Then what would Jill do? Call Ryan and tell him their date is off because her parents won't let her go? That would be so geeky!"

"But how can I go out on a date without them knowing?" asked Jill. She started playing nervously with the end of her dark braid.

"We'll help," Nikki promised. "You can say you're doing something with us. You've just *got* to go on this date. I mean, it's cooler than cool, Jill. But you have to tell us all about it afterward."

"Every single detail," agreed Danielle.

"You guys are the best," Jill said. "I really mean it. Sneaking out to go on a date with Ryan would be impossible without your help." Jill didn't feel good about lying to her parents, but what could she do?

"There's no way I'm going to pass up a chance like this," Jill continued. "And anyway, my parents have to get used to me having more freedom. After all, I've been away from home for months, and I never have to ask them for permission when I go out at the Academy."

"Where are those sundaes?" Tori said. "I'm starved!"

"They've got to realize I'm getting older now," Jill went on. "At the Academy you have to take on lots of responsibility without your parents watching over you. It's not like being at home and skating for Silver Blades. Mom and Dad will just have to accept that I need my independence."

"Here you are, ladies," the waitress said. She began passing out the dishes of ice cream that would soon become incredibly rich, gloppy sundaes once the five girls finished layering on their favorite toppings.

"Brain food," Danielle said, grinning at her dish.

"Don't tell my mother about this," Tori said. "She's always telling me to eat like an athlete. I'm so sick of carrots, apples, and whole-grain bread with low-fat cream cheese."

"Even top athletes need time off every so often," Jill said. "But you wouldn't believe how some of the girls at the Academy work out and stick to really strict diets. Some of them never take a break—like my roommate, Bronya."

"Really?" Danielle said.

Jill nodded. "I didn't know what hard work was until I went to the Academy." She jammed her spoon into the ice cream. "I'm going to love every bite of this," she declared. " 'Cause I worked hard for it."

"Let's hit Canady's when we're finished and try on clothes," Tori suggested, changing the subject.

"Good idea," Jill agreed. "My mom gave me forty dollars to spend on clothes. I'd like to find something to wear Friday night."

"We'll help you find something great," Danielle promised. "After all, this is your first real date."

"My first real date!" Jill said dreamily, and a chill ran through her that had nothing to do with ice cream.

"So, what sort of look do you want for Friday night, Jill?" Tori was the fashion expert in the group, and she took charge immediately once the girls were inside Canady's. "Sophisticated? Elegant? Party girl? What?"

"I want to look sophisticated but fun—and not too dressy. I want to look like myself, only better," Jill said. Then, glancing sheepishly at her friends, she added, "I want to look older than thirteen."

"How about this?" Haley asked, holding up a black suede vest with fringe. "Is this wicked or what?"

Tori made a face. "It's too Western," she said.

"It just isn't Jill," Nikki added.

"Jill needs something red," declared Danielle.

Tori rolled her eyes. "As if Jill doesn't have enough red stuff in her wardrobe already. How about switching your favorite color to pink, Jill?" Tori asked, holding up a pink blouse with puffy sleeves and a wide collar.

Just the thing, Jill told herself, for Tori!

Jill shook her head. "It's nice, Tori. But it would look great on you, not me."

"Can I help you girls?" a salesgirl who looked as if she was in her late teens asked.

"No thanks," Tori said quickly.

"Wait a minute," said Danielle. "Maybe we could use a little help." Danielle quickly explained what the girls were after.

The salesgirl smiled and nodded. "You can all go in that changing room over there and I'll bring a few things for your friend to try on," she said. "By the way, my name is Andrea."

"I'm going to sit down," Nikki said, heading toward the dressing room. "All that ice cream kind of made me sleepy. I'm glad I don't eat like that all the time."

"I just hope I fit into my regular size," Jill joked. She and the others followed Nikki.

A few minutes later Andrea returned with several

sweaters, tops, leggings, dresses, and skirts. Every piece was something Jill might have picked out herself.

"You look great in anything, Jill," Danielle said. "You're so lucky you're naturally slim."

"Too bad I have only forty dollars to spend." Jill lifted the tag on the red velvet top that she had tried on. "Oops!" she said, letting the tag drop again. "This is way too expensive."

"It's kind of dressy anyway," Haley declared. "I thought you wanted something more casual."

Jill took off the top and, after checking the tag on a turquoise Lycra T, she tried it on. She turned first to the left and then to the right in front of the three-way mirror. Then she faced her friends. "What do you guys think? It's not too expensive and I think it'll look good with my black jeans."

"You're going to wear jeans on your date?" asked Tori, sounding horrified.

"Why not?" Jill looked at herself in the mirror again. Suddenly the top didn't look very special. But Jill didn't feel like letting Tori know she'd discouraged her.

Tori shook her head. "Jeans aren't very sophisticated," she said. "I thought you wanted to look sophisticated."

"I do," Jill agreed, wishing Tori would stop acting like such a know-it-all. "But I don't want to overdress for this date either. That wouldn't be cool."

"I suppose not," Tori allowed grudgingly. "But you're going to wear your hair loose, aren't you? At least do that."

Jill shrugged. She did plan to wear her hair down, but she didn't want Tori to think it was because she had suggested it. "I haven't decided yet," she said vaguely.

"Then it's settled," Nikki said. "Jill's buying the top she likes. Now let's go!" Nikki stood up and stretched.

"Maybe I should get this fuzzy sweater instead." Jill picked up a red mohair sweater. "Which one is more romantic?" she asked her friends. "Maybe I should go for romantic instead of sophisticated."

"The sweater," voted Danielle. Haley agreed. Nikki nodded wearily. But Tori stubbornly refused to vote.

"Then I'll go with the sweater," Jill decided, not looking at Tori.

Jill took the sweater to the register, and after the sale was rung up, she asked Andrea for the time.

"About four-thirty, I think," Andrea said cheerfully.

"Oh, no!" Jill cried. She looked at her friends, who stood nearby, waiting. "I'm supposed to be back at the Arena! I'm in big trouble!"

7

"**T**hanks for the ride, Dad," Jill said early Thursday morning as her father pulled up in front of the Ice Arena.

"Don't mention it," Mr. Wong said. He looked at his wristwatch. "It's only ten after five. We're early."

"Good," Jill said with determination. She'd wanted to be early. She'd missed nearly an hour of her ice time yesterday afternoon by getting back late from the mall. Even though her parents never found out, Jill felt worse than she thought she would. She felt she'd let her parents down, especially since they had to pay for the time she'd missed. Now, she told herself, I have a chance to make it up to them. She smiled at her father.

Mr. Wong patted Jill's knee affectionately. "You're a very hard worker, Jill. I'm proud of you."

Jill avoided his eyes. She didn't feel she deserved her father's praise. Not today anyway. Not after being late for practice, but that wasn't the only reason. She thought about her date with Ryan the following night, and how she wasn't going to tell her parents about it. Pushing it out of her mind, she said a quick good-bye and hopped out of the minivan.

Jill was glad no one was in the locker room. It felt good to be alone for a little while. Back at the Ice Academy I have too much time alone, she told herself. But now that I'm home, I miss the peace and quiet.

She pulled on her red-and-black unitard. After carefully lacing her skates, she hurried out of the locker room. Stopping at the barrier, she yanked off her guards and skated out onto the ice.

Jill loved the feel of freshly groomed ice. It's so smooth and crisp, she told herself. It's like skating on glass. The air felt cool and moist on her cheeks. The ice even smelled good as her skates carved into it. This morning the ice is almost as nice as the ice back at the Academy, she decided. She circled the rink once, twice, three times, and her black hair flew straight out behind her. She glided almost effortlessly, feeling as if she were airborne.

Out of the corner of her eye Jill could see other skaters arriving. But she still didn't slow down to see if any of the new arrivals were her friends.

"Jill!" a voice called out. It sounded like Danielle. But Jill didn't want to stop and chat. She wanted to keep skating. She decided to try a triple toe loop before the ice got too crowded.

Focus, focus, concentrate, Jill told herself. She skated forward, gently leaning her weight on her right foot. Then she quickly turned backward and tapped her left toe into the ice. Scooping up her arms, she catapulted into the air. I'm flying, she told herself as she whirled effortlessly. Her landing was firm.

Applause exploded from all around Jill, and she felt a thrill rush through her limbs. She couldn't stop smiling as she prepared for her next move—her double axel. She bent her left knee. Her arms were stretched backward. For a second she wondered if Tori was watching.

In a single movement Jill brought her arms forward and her right leg close to her body, thrusting herself into the air. Pulling her arms in tight and crossing her ankles for speed, she turned two and a half revolutions.

"Go, Jill!" someone yelled from off the ice. She noticed that it sounded like a boy's voice, but she didn't let it break her concentration. "Go!" Obligingly, she performed a double salchow. Again there was applause. Jill did a triple flip and then a double lutz. The applause grew louder. She felt totally exhilarated.

Finally, out of breath, she slowed down, circling the Arena a couple of times to cool down. Then she skated to the center of the rink, where a crowd of Silver Blades skaters, including Tori and Danielle, waited.

"Hey, Jill," Tori said. "What did you have for breakfast this morning? Rocket fuel?"

"You're sooo good, Jill," gushed Kelly O'Reilly, one of the younger skaters in Silver Blades. "Will I ever be as good as you are?"

"Sure. It just takes tons of practice," Jill advised Kelly as she caught her breath.

"Speaking of practice, how did things go when you finally got here yesterday?" Danielle asked. "My grandmother was happy to give you a ride."

"Okay, I guess. Your grandmother saved my life. I'm glad she could pick us up or I would have waited forever for the bus and missed even more of practice," Jill said. "I'm just mad that I didn't pay more attention to the time, but I was having too much fun hanging out with you guys. I don't get to shop like that in Denver with my tight schedule at the Academy."

"But now you're set for your big date Friday," Danielle said.

"Everything's set for Saturday too," Tori added. "Mom said it was okay to move the slumber party to then. What do you guys want to do? Rent movies? Make our own pizza? Talk about Jill's date?"

"Sounds like fun," Jill said. "Only I'm not sure I want to tell you guys everything about my date. Some things are private, you know," she said with a sly smile.

"You can't keep secrets from us," Tori declared. "And speaking of secrets, I want to know all the secrets they've been telling you at the Academy, Jill. Like how to get all that height on your triple toe loop, for instance."

"Are you asking me for skating advice?" Jill asked. She knew she could teach Tori a few things she'd learned, but she didn't want her getting mad again for trying to help.

"Well, yeah," Tori said. "What I really want are secrets. They must pass along little tidbits at the Academy. You know, one or two things that make all the difference."

Jill shook her head. "Sorry, Tori, I don't really have any tidbits to tell you. They just make us work really hard. There aren't any secrets, you just have to practice, practice, practice. You should know that by now yourself."

"Come on, Jill," Tori pleaded as if she thought Jill was holding out on her. "They must have taught you something new that we haven't heard before. After all, it is the fabulous International Ice Academy."

"Well, I can't tell you any secrets because there aren't any," Jill said again. "But I could watch what you're doing and give you some advice."

"Will you watch me too?" Danielle asked.

"Sure," Jill agreed. "I'd be glad to watch both of you. But first you both have to promise not to get mad at me for being honest with you."

But before either Danielle or Tori could reply, Haley skated over to them from the boards.

"Jill!" Haley said excitedly. "A guy came up to me

when I got here a little while ago. He said he was here to see you and asked me if I knew you." Haley grabbed Jill's arm and started pulling her toward the side of the rink.

"Wait," Jill said, yanking her arm away. She had been the target of Haley's jokes more than once and wasn't about to fall for another one now. "What is this all about, Haley?" she asked suspiciously. Jill glanced at Tori and Danielle to see if they might be in on Haley's joke, but they just looked curious.

"This is no joke, Jill. Honest," Haley insisted. "I talked to him myself. He's really cute. Long brown hair. Brown puppy-dog eyes. Does that ring a bell?"

"Ryan!" Tori and Danielle exclaimed at the same time.

"He didn't say his name," Haley admitted. "But he sure looks like the guy you described as your big date!"

"Go check it out, Jill," Danielle urged. "And don't forget, if it is Ryan, I want to meet him."

"We all want to meet him," Tori corrected her.

Still not totally convinced Haley wasn't playing a practical joke on her, Jill skated to the other end of the rink. As she neared the barrier, Ryan stood up and waved at her.

"What are you doing here?" she demanded, shocked to see him at the rink.

"Aren't you going to say hi?" he asked. "After all, I did get up really early just so I could see you skate."

"You did?" Jill smiled. If Ryan had come to the Arena

this early just to see her, that meant he'd been thinking about her. And maybe that meant he really liked her.

Ryan nodded. "I saw you skate."

"You did?" she asked again, thinking that he looked even better than she'd remembered.

"I don't really know much about figure skating, but you looked good. Really good. Didn't you hear me cheering for you?" he asked, raking his fingers through his long hair.

So that was the guy's voice I heard, Jill thought.

"You must be the best skater here," Ryan said. "Everybody stopped to watch you."

"Well," Jill said shyly, "I am the only one in Silver Blades who goes to the International Ice Academy, so I guess you're right." She wasn't used to getting such a nice compliment from a guy as cute as Ryan, and it made her self-conscious to admit that she was good.

"Ahem!" Someone on Jill's right pretended to clear her throat. Jill turned and saw that Nikki had arrived while she'd been talking with Ryan. Now all four of her friends stood a few feet behind her. Had they heard her bragging to Ryan? Well, she told herself, so what if they did? What I said was true, and I worked hard to get good. Tori and Danielle wouldn't have begged me for advice if they didn't think I was good too.

"Come here," Jill said, waving her friends over. They skated slowly toward her in a clump. When they stopped next to Jill, Haley mumbled something, and they all giggled. Jill looked quickly at Ryan. Does he think my friends are immature? she wondered. But he was smiling at them in a friendly way.

"This is Ryan," Jill said, and her friends giggled again. She frowned at them, but they were too busy gawking at Ryan to notice. Jill felt embarrassed.

"Hi," Ryan said. He flipped his long hair back with a jerk of his head.

"Remember me?" Haley said. "I'm the one who told you where Jill was."

Ryan nodded. "Thanks," he said. He gave his hair another flip. He's nervous, Jill realized. But who wouldn't be? Then Jill looked at her friends. Suddenly she saw them as silly little girls without a clue about how to act around an older boy. She wished they'd go away, but she knew they wouldn't. At least not until they'd been introduced.

"That's Haley," Jill said, hoping to satisfy them so they'd leave. "And this is Tori . . . Nikki . . . and Danielle."

"Jill's told us all about you," Haley blurted out.

Jill noticed that Ryan actually blushed, and she groaned silently. Couldn't her friends just act their age?

"I just told them how I met you, that's all," Jill said quickly to Ryan. "They wanted to meet you too, and now they have," she added pointedly, hoping her friends would get the hint. But no one made a move to go.

"Do you really have a dog named Groucho?" Haley persisted. She leaned her elbows on the barrier and put her head in her hands. "That's a goofy name. How did you think of it?"

"Groucho was one of the Marx brothers," Ryan explained. "You know who the Marx brothers are, don't you?"

"Not really," Haley said with a shrug. "Do they live in Seneca Hills?"

"They're a comedy team," Nikki told Haley. "We have a bunch of their old movies on video. My dad thinks they're great."

Suddenly Jill was aware of someone skating up to her. She turned and saw Kathy Bart stop right beside her. "What's going on here?" Kathy asked.

"A friend came to watch me skate," Jill said quickly.

"Then let's skate!" Kathy said. "Come on, girls. Get going!"

Jill cringed. It was so embarrassing being treated like a baby by Kathy, especially in front of Ryan. She was sure he must think they all needed a baby-sitter. But when Jill looked at him, he just smiled and shrugged.

"I'll wait for you," he said. "We can catch some breakfast together when you're finished."

Jill watched her friends skate after Kathy. Then she glanced at the clock on the wall and saw that she still had quite a bit of ice time left. Quickly she made up her mind.

"You don't need to wait," she told Ryan. "I don't take lessons here anymore. And besides, I'm on vacation. Let's go now!"

"How do you feel about Breakfast Burritos?" Ryan asked after he and Jill left the Ice Arena. Jill had changed out of her unitard and into faded jeans, her Ice Academy sweatshirt, and a light jacket. If she had known Ryan would show up, she would have worn something else. But Ryan was wearing beat-up jeans and a flannel shirt too, so she guessed it was okay.

"I've never had a Breakfast Burrito," Jill admitted. "But I'd like to try one."

"Okay. I know Burger Buddy is open. Sometimes I stop there in the morning for a burrito while I'm out walking Groucho. They're good—like an omelette wrapped up in a tortilla."

"Sounds great," Jill said.

"It's a few blocks that way. You don't mind walking, do you?" Ryan asked. "I mean, I don't have a car. I can't drive yet, at least not by myself. I just got my learner's permit."

"I don't mind walking," Jill assured him. "In fact, I like walking." She took a deep breath. "It smells different here than it does in Colorado. It's damper or something. You can smell the earth. I like it."

Ryan smiled and nodded. "I like it too. In fact, walking or hiking is just about my favorite thing to do. Ever been rock climbing?"

Jill shook her head. "Skating takes up most of my time. I don't get to try a lot of other stuff."

When they reached Burger Buddy, Ryan ordered while Jill found them a booth. They were just beginning to unwrap their burritos when Ryan suddenly jumped up and started waving.

"A couple of friends of mine just walked in," he told Jill after he sat back down. "The guy is my lab partner in bio. He's here with his girlfriend."

"Hey, dude," a short guy with sandy brown hair said a moment later. He set his tray on their table and slapped Ryan on the back. "What's up?"

Ryan laughed. "Breakfast, man. Have a seat."

"Okay." The boy waved at a blond girl. "Over here, Cindy."

"This is Nate," Ryan said as the boy sat down. "And that's Cindy."

Jill smiled at the blond girl as she sat down. "Hi, Cindy," she said. "My name's Jill."

Slipping her arm around Nate's waist, Cindy fixed her blue eyes on Jill. "I haven't seen you before. You don't go to Seneca Hills High, do you?"

"No," Jill said. "I don't live in Seneca Hills anymore."

"Jill goes to a skating school in Colorado. She's just here visiting her family," Ryan explained. Jill wondered nervously whether he'd mention that she was only thirteen and really a seventh-grader. But he didn't.

"Oh, wow!" Cindy said, raising her eyebrows and giving Jill an admiring look. "You must be good."

"She's awesome," Ryan said, smiling at Jill.

"So, what are you two doing out this early?" Cindy asked them.

"I went to the Ice Arena this morning to watch Jill skate," Ryan told her. "I sort of surprised her. Didn't I, Jill?"

Jill laughed. "Totally!"

"How about you guys?" Ryan asked. "Why are you out so early?"

"We've been in line since five-thirty for tickets to the Aluminum Pyros concert," Cindy said. "They're performing here next month, you know."

"Cool," Ryan said.

"Anyway, the line is forever. Some people even camped out overnight," Cindy explained. "So the guys next to us said they'd hold our place while we ate if we'd do the same for them." She shrugged. "So here we are."

"You two want tickets?" Nate asked. "We can get four, no problem."

Ryan looked at Jill hopefully. "Want to?" he asked.

"I do, but I can't. I'm going back to Denver next week," she reminded him.

"Oh, yeah," Ryan said, sounding disappointed. Jill felt bad. She wished she could go to the concert, and realized for the first time that it might be hard to leave next week after meeting Ryan.

"Hey, no sweat. We can double some other time," Nate said.

Ryan brightened. "That's a great idea! What are you guys doing Friday night? You've got a car, right?"

Nate nodded. "Right. How about a movie or something?"

"Sure," Cindy said as she stood up. "But we'd better get going now. We promised those people we wouldn't take long."

"Want to walk over to the Civic Center with us?" Nate asked. "You guys can keep us from getting too bored while we wait in line."

Ryan looked at Jill and waited for her answer. She liked Ryan's friends. Cindy was nice, and she seemed more mature than most of Jill's friends. Nate was even old enough to drive a car. Jill thought back to her giggling friends whom Ryan had met at the rink. It's time I got to know some new people, she told herself.

"It sounds cool," she said to Ryan.

"We're outta here," Ryan said, handing Jill her jacket.

8

"**I**s that you, Jill?" Mrs. Wong called out from the kitchen as Jill walked in the door. She had left Ryan, Cindy, and Nate at the Civic Center and caught the bus home.

"Yes, Mom," Jill called back. "I'm home."

"Come here right now," Mrs. Wong said. "I need to talk to you."

Oh, no, Jill thought as she made her way to the kitchen. I'd better think fast. She's going to ask where I've been.

"It's almost two o'clock," Mrs. Wong told Jill as she furiously chopped celery by the sink. "I expected you home at noon. I thought Danielle's grandmother was giving you a ride. But when I called over there, I found out she hadn't even seen you."

"Sorry, Mom. I hung out at the rink for a while. I

didn't think you'd mind," Jill said. She hated lying, but she couldn't let her mother know she'd left the rink early and missed even more of the ice time her parents had paid for. And there was no way she could let her mother find out she'd been with Ryan.

"I wished you'd called me," Mrs. Wong said. She pushed the chopped celery away with her knife and set a green pepper down in its place. "Next time please let me know if you plan to be late."

"I'm sorry," Jill said again. "I'm not used to reporting everything I do to you anymore. I forgot."

"Next time," Mrs. Wong said without looking up at Jill, "don't forget."

I can't believe this, Jill thought as she headed for the stairs. They're treating me like a two-year-old. What do they think I do when I'm at the Academy? Stay out till the sun comes up? Maybe I should wear a beeper. That way they can keep track of me twenty-four hours a day.

She was hoping to be alone in the bedroom so that she could try on her clothes for her double date tomorrow. It would be fun to hang out with Cindy and Nate. When it had finally leaked out that Jill was only thirteen, Cindy had even said she never would have guessed it because Jill was so mature. Mature. Jill smiled as she reached for the knob on her bedroom door. Cindy is so cool. So is Nate. But Ryan is the best of all! she told herself as she opened the door. Instead of having the room to herself as she'd hoped, Jill discovered Kristi reading on her bed.

"Tori called about a half hour ago," Kristi said, looking up from her book. "She sounded mad."

Jill threw herself on the other twin bed. "Tori's always mad about something. She's so immature."

"Don't you like Tori anymore?" Kristi asked.

"I guess I like her," Jill said with a shrug. "I just wish she'd grow up a little."

"Jill!" Mrs. Wong called from downstairs. "Telephone."

"Okay, Mom," Jill called back as she got up from the bed and went to the hallway phone. It was Tori.

"Why did you leave the rink so early this morning?" Tori demanded as soon as Jill picked up the phone and said hello. "I thought you were going to give Danielle and me some advice."

"I'm sorry. I guess I forgot with all the excitement this morning," Jill whispered. She didn't want her mother to overhear anything. Especially after she'd just lied about where she'd been.

"Someone said you left with Ryan," Tori said.

"I did," Jill said. She carried the phone to the railing and peered over. She didn't see her mother, but that didn't mean her mother couldn't hear every word. "Look, I can't talk about it now," she whispered.

"Where did you two go?" Tori asked.

"Tori, not now. Anyway, I've got to run. My mother's calling me," Jill lied.

"Don't you want to know what I thought of him before you go?" Tori asked.

"Oh, all right," Jill said, knowing it was easier to

give in than to get rid of Tori. "Then I really have to go."

"I think he's gorgeous," Tori said eagerly. "Everyone does."

Suddenly Jill felt a little more interested in what Tori had to say. "You do?" she said.

"Totally. Did he say any more about Friday?"

"He did. But like I said, now's not a good time for me to talk," Jill said. "If someone hears me, I'm dead." Jill nervously switched the phone from her right ear to her left ear. "I'm beginning to wonder how I'll ever get away with . . . you know what."

"Your date? Don't worry, Jill," Tori said. "I've got the best plan for you."

"You have? Like what?" Jill asked eagerly.

"I thought you had to hang up," Tori said.

"I do, but tell me anyway—quick," Jill demanded.

"Okay. Here it is. You bring the stuff you need for your date to your afternoon practice tomorrow. You tell your parents it's because you're going out with all of us to the movies after skating. You get ready for your date at the Ice Arena. Then you have Ryan meet you there instead of at your house."

"You know," Jill said excitedly, "that just might work."

"How do I look, Danielle?" Jill asked as she checked herself out in the mirror in the locker room at the Ice

Arena. It was Friday, and she'd just showered and dressed and blow-dried her hair. Holding a lipstick in one hand and her hairbrush in the other, Jill flipped her long black hair behind her shoulders. "Do you think I'm wearing too much makeup? Do you think this sweater looks okay? Should I braid my hair?"

"Whoa, Jill! Slow down," Danielle said. "You look great. I've never seen you so nervous about the way you look before."

After touching up her lipstick, Jill turned away from the mirror and faced Danielle. "This is the first time I've gotten the chance to look really nice for Ryan. The other two times I was caught by surprise, and I looked kind of grungy."

Danielle shook her head. "You've got nothing to worry about, Jill. You always look nice, even when you look grungy. Ryan must think so too, or he wouldn't have asked you out."

Jill smiled. "Thanks, Dani."

"So he's meeting you here?" Danielle asked.

Jill turned back to the mirror and slipped a red headband over her glossy hair. "When he called last night I told him to meet me here at seven. I was so afraid one of my parents would hear me when I was talking to him." Jill patted her stomach. "If you ever decide to diet again, Dani, just try lying to your parents and sneaking around like this. I bet I lost five pounds just today. I haven't been able to eat a thing because I've been so nervous."

"Well, stop worrying. Everything's okay. It's almost

seven now, and he should be here any minute. Then you can go out and have the time of your life. Do you want me to go see if he's here yet?"

"I'll go," Jill said, picking up her shoulder bag.

"Want me to come with you?" Danielle offered.

"Actually," Jill said, "would you mind not coming with me? I don't want Ryan to think I'm some little seventh-grader who can't meet my date by myself."

"But you are a seventh-grader," Danielle said, frowning. "So am I. What's wrong with that?"

"Well, I mean, Ryan thinks I'm more sophisticated than that, you know?" Jill explained. She didn't mean to hurt Danielle's feelings. She really appreciated all her help. And of all her friends, Danielle was the most grown-up. Jill hoped that she would understand.

"It's okay if you want to meet him on your own," Danielle said. She smiled at Jill and started stuffing the makeup, which she'd brought along for Jill, back into her little bag.

Jill gave Danielle a quick hug. "I knew you'd understand," she said. "Oh, I almost forgot, Dani. Yesterday I was going to show you some things I'd learned at the Academy, but I didn't get a chance. I promise I'll help you tomorrow. Okay?"

"Okay," Danielle replied.

Jill dashed out of the locker room, saying over her shoulder, "I'll call you tomorrow."

Jill spotted Ryan standing by the snack bar. He saw her too and waved as he started walking toward her.

"Wow," Ryan said when they met up. "You look great."

"Thanks. So do you." And he did too. Like Jill, Ryan had on jeans and a sweater, only his sweater was blue instead of red.

"Nate and Cindy should be here by now," Ryan said. "Let's go out and see." Ryan took Jill's hand and they walked outside together.

Jill had never held hands with a boy before, and she felt a little thrill as she gripped his warm hand.

"There they are," Ryan said, pointing across the parking lot at a blue VW bug. As soon as they climbed into the backseat of Nate's car, Jill asked Cindy if she'd gotten the tickets she'd been standing in line for yesterday.

"Yup," Cindy said. "We got them all right. We're way up in the balcony, but lots of people didn't get tickets at all."

"Lucky for you," Jill said.

"It's too bad you won't be around for the concert," Cindy said. "Nate and I are giving a preconcert party. It's going to be a major event."

"Well, tonight is a major event too," Jill said, surprised at her own words. She smiled at Ryan.

"So what movie are we going to see?" Ryan asked.

"I vote for *Swamp Creature*," Nate said, making his voice sound eerie. He revved the engine of the car, then added, "It's at the mall."

"I just hope it's not too gross," Cindy said.

"If it's like the original black-and-white version, it's scary only if you live in a swamp," Ryan assured her. "I don't think the creature can survive in the air more than a minute or two."

"Hey!" Nate protested. "You're giving the plot away!"

"How about you, Jill?" Ryan said. "Are you into horror movies?"

"I love them!" Jill declared.

"That makes it unanimous!" Ryan cheered. "*Swamp Creature* wins!"

Jill laughed and Ryan squeezed her hand. The truth was, she didn't care what movie she saw. She was just happy to be out with Ryan and his friends for the night. So happy that for the moment she didn't care that she had lied to her parents to go out. This was going to be one of the best nights of her life, and nothing was going to spoil it. It was more than she'd ever dreamed her vacation could be.

"So," Cindy said as soon as the girls were alone in the rest room at the theater. "Do you like him?"

Jill tilted her head to one side and nodded.

"That's good, because I can tell he likes you," Cindy said. "You're the first girl he's asked out in Seneca Hills that I know of."

"Really?" Jill said, feeling flattered.

"Yeah," Cindy said, pulling a tube of lipstick out of her shoulder bag. "A lot of girls have been asking about him. You know—wondering if he's going out with any-body. Believe me, Ryan can go out with anyone he wants to."

Wow! Jill said to herself.

Cindy twisted her lipstick up. "This is called tawny peach," she said, showing the color to Jill. "You prob-ably look better in red than orange." Jill nodded again. She didn't want to tell Cindy that she owned only one tube of lipstick and that the lipstick she was wearing now wasn't even hers.

"There, all done," Cindy said as she spread one last stroke of tawny peach on her lower lip. "Time to join the guys."

Nate and Ryan were playing a video game in the lobby when the girls came out. Ryan was at the con-trols, while Nate held two jumbo buckets of popcorn. Jill was about to walk over to them when she spotted Danielle's brother Nicholas and a bunch of his hockey buddies at a video game right beside Ryan's. The last thing she needed just then was to have Nicholas see her.

"What's wrong, Jill?" Cindy said.

"Oh, nothing." Jill edged slowly back to the water fountain. "Just thirsty." She couldn't tell Cindy what was really wrong.

"We'd better get the guys and go in," Cindy said.

"You go," Jill said. "I'll get a drink." After Cindy walked away, Nicholas and his friends headed toward Jill. She ducked her head over the fountain and took a long drink. Jill was relieved that the boys never noticed her. When Cindy returned with Ryan and Nate, she felt she could relax again. The foursome headed into the theater.

"Hey, Jill!" someone yelled when they got halfway down the aisle. Jill knew exactly who it was, but she didn't answer. She wanted to duck and hide but she couldn't—it would be totally immature. Instead, she pretended she just hadn't heard. She slipped to the other side of Ryan and continued down the aisle.

"Isn't that Nicholas Panati?" Cindy asked, tapping Jill on the arm.

Now Jill had to look—there was no avoiding it. She glanced over at Nicholas, who was sitting in the middle row of seats with his friends. Nicholas was looking right at her. When their eyes met, he waved. Jill waved back.

"You know him?" Cindy said, sounding impressed. When Jill nodded, Cindy added, "He's supposed to be a really good hockey player. He played on the varsity team this year, you know. Our team was third in the state too."

Jill just smiled and nodded again. What if he mentions this to my mother? she thought, biting a nail as they continued down the aisle. But why would he? she reasoned. Anyway, she'd told her mother she was going to the movies tonight. And Nicholas might not mention whom she was with if he did tell anybody. It wasn't so strange to see her in a theater with a couple of her friends. Calm down, she told herself. You're on vacation and this is your first date. Enjoy it. She settled into a seat next to Ryan and munched on some of the popcorn he offered her.

Swamp Creature turned out to be just the kind of movie Jill loved—a little gross but not really scary. After it was over, Nate said, "Where to now? Pizza or ice cream?"

"Ice cream," Cindy said as they left the theater.

But Jill didn't want to press her luck. Running into Nicholas might not turn into a big deal. But her next run-in with someone else she knew might not go so well.

"I'm sorry to be a drag, but I have to be at the rink at five-thirty tomorrow morning," she said, making her voice sound as apologetic as she could. "I have to get home to bed."

"But it's not even ten-thirty," Ryan protested. "And it's Friday night."

Jill felt terrible about disappointing him, but she didn't have a choice. She shrugged. "That's the price a person pays for being a serious athlete, I guess."

"Even a serious athlete has to have fun," Ryan said. "It's your vacation. Live it up!"

"But, Ryan," Cindy said. "She's got to get up before the sun rises."

"Yeah, I guess you're right," Ryan said.

"We could walk home instead of riding with Nate and Cindy," Jill suggested hopefully. Ryan had said he liked walking and Jill was sure that at ten-thirty at night, walking home from the theater, they wouldn't run into anyone her parents knew.

"Okay," Ryan agreed. But he still sounded disappointed.

"So long, you two," Nate said, slipping his arm around Cindy.

"Yeah," Cindy said. "So long."

"Thanks," Jill said. "I had a great time tonight. I hope I see you again sometime."

Then Jill was alone with Ryan. "I'm sorry I've got to go home so early," she said. "You aren't too mad, are you?"

"I'm not mad at all," Ryan said, taking hold of her hand.

They walked in silence for a while. Jill liked being with Ryan. It was odd how being with him was both exciting and peaceful. Before she knew it, they'd reached Browndale Avenue. Jill stopped walking.

"What's up?" Ryan asked, giving her a puzzled look.

"This is my street," she said, nodding at the green sign that hung from the streetlight.

"I know," Ryan said. "I called you last night, remember? I saw your address in the phone book, 405 Browndale Avenue. Which house is yours?"

Jill knew she couldn't let Ryan walk her all the way to the door. Her parents thought she'd gone to a movie with her girlfriends. If she showed up at the door with Ryan, they'd lose it. She had to tell Ryan something. But all she could think of was the truth. She had had enough of lying.

Taking a big breath, she blurted out, "My parents don't know I'm out with you tonight."

"What do you mean?" Ryan asked. "Where do they think you are?"

"Oh, they know I went to a movie. But they think I went with those girls you met at the rink." Jill avoided Ryan's eyes. "I didn't tell them I was going on a date with you." As she spoke, Jill couldn't believe how dumb she sounded.

"Why would you lie?" Ryan asked.

"I was afraid they'd say no," Jill said. "And I really wanted to go out with you. You probably think this is all really stupid. I mean, you're in high school and everything."

"No," he said, putting his hands on her shoulders. "Not stupid. I think it's nice that you like me that much, you know, enough to lie like that. Would you go out with me again?" he asked, looking into her eyes.

"Yes," Jill said a little breathlessly. "I'd love to."

Then, before she knew what was happening, Ryan's lips brushed hers. Her knees wobbled slightly, and for a second she forgot how to breathe.

She drew away and looked into his brown eyes. He smiled at her and she smiled back. Then she gave him another kiss—a quick good-night kiss—and said, "I have to go now."

"I'll call you," he said.

Jill turned and ran up the sidewalk toward her house. When she got to the front door, she paused with her hand on the knob. She looked back and saw Ryan disappearing around the corner of the block.

"He kissed me!" she whispered. She closed her eyes and held on to the feeling for a moment. "He kissed me!"

"**S**o tell us everything, Jill," Danielle said early Saturday morning as the girls got ready to skate. "My brother said he saw you at the theater. He said that he didn't even know it was you at first because you were with a bunch of high-school kids."

Jill stopped lacing her skates and looked up sharply at Danielle. "I hope he doesn't go tell the whole world that he saw me with Ryan last night," she said. "You know I could get in big trouble for that." Jill's parents hadn't asked any questions when she'd returned from her date, and Jill was hoping to keep it that way.

"Don't worry," Danielle said. "Nicholas never talks to grown-ups unless he absolutely has to."

"So tell us, did you have fun?" Haley asked Jill as she slipped a short black skating skirt on over her black leotard. She wiggled her eyebrows at Jill. "And, most important of all, did he kiss you?"

Jill felt her cheeks color and quickly bent over her laces, pretending she hadn't heard Haley's question. Bronya would never ask a question like that, she thought. I'm starting to miss the privacy I had at the Academy.

"Come on, Jill," Tori said, crossing the locker room and standing over her. "Why are you being so secretive about your date? We're dying to know what happened."

"Maybe I'm just not ready to talk about it," Jill said. She finished tying her skates and stood up.

"You've never kept secrets from us before," Tori said. "Will you tell us about it tonight at my party?"

Jill shrugged. She had always liked sharing everything with her friends. But now something stopped her from telling them about her date with Ryan. It had been a special night, and for now she wanted to hold on to that feeling and keep it private. If she told everyone about the kiss, it wouldn't be hers any longer.

"I'm sure I can think of something to tell you by tonight," Jill finally said, hoping to satisfy them.

"At least tell us what movie you saw," Nikki insisted.

"She saw *Swamp Creature,*" Danielle said. "I know because she saw the same movie my brother did. Nicholas also told me he spotted Jill holding hands with Ryan as she left the theater."

"Oo-la-la!" Nikki, Haley, and Tori sang out.

Jill laughed in spite of herself. "I can't believe it. You guys are so incredibly immature!"

"Hey!" Kathy Bart said, storming into the locker room. "What are you girls doing in here? Your lesson time started five minutes ago, Tori. You better get out there. Mr. Weiler's on the warpath. And Alex and I have been waiting for you for ten minutes now, Nikki. The rest of you better get out there fast and start warming up."

Jill smiled as she hurried out to the ice with the other girls. She wouldn't have thought she'd ever be happy to hear Kathy lose her temper. But today she was. Saved by Sarge, she told herself.

Once she was warmed up, Jill skated to the corner of the rink to work on some footwork combinations. But she couldn't concentrate and gave up after a few minutes. She needed something more exciting, like flashy freestyle moves. She noticed that Jessica McVay and Kelly O'Reilly, two of the youngest members of Silver Blades, were watching her closely. Jill smiled and waved at them. Jumps and spins will be more fun for Jessica and Melissa to watch too, Jill decided.

First, she'd do her double axel. She circled the rink for speed and picked a spot. She turned two and a half revolutions and landed perfectly. Then she practiced a change-foot sit spin. Seeing that the younger girls were still watching her encouraged Jill to do her best. She performed a double lutz next. As she glided backward past the younger girls, she smiled again. She remembered when she had looked up to older, more skilled skaters. I guess things haven't changed, she thought. Only now I am the one they look up to.

When she finally slowed down to catch her breath, Jill saw that Tori had finished her lesson with Mr. Weiler. He was coaching Danielle now, and Tori was working alone on her double axel, practicing it over and over again.

Jill watched Tori make several attempts and could see that she still hadn't achieved the height or speed required for the difficult spin. Tori still looked awkward when she pulled her arms and legs in too. Also, her rotations were forced. Jill skated over to talk to her.

"Tori," Jill said. "Hi."

"Hi," Tori returned breathlessly. She pushed the damp blond curls from her forehead with the back of her hand. "Did you see me land those double axels? I'm not falling at all anymore. I'm really getting it now."

"Remember the other day when I said I'd help you?" Jill asked, thinking that now was a good time to do a favor for her friend.

Tori nodded eagerly. "I sure do. You said you'd tell me what they've been teaching you at the Ice Academy."

"Well, I just watched you now and I saw that your timing is off. Not enough to make you fall, but enough to keep you from looking as good as you could."

Tori's blue eyes narrowed. "Oh?" she said. "My timing?"

"Yeah," Jill said. "You're rotating your shoulders okay now. But it looks like you're dropping your free arm on the landing."

"Why didn't Mr. Weiler tell me these things?" Tori said. "I mean, he's my coach."

"I don't know," Jill said. "All I know is that this is what we were taught at the Academy. Watch me and I'll show you what I mean."

Jill circled the rink a couple of times for speed. She found herself dodging other skaters, including Danielle, who was having a lesson. When she was right in front of Tori, Jill decided she'd perform the double axel the way Tori had been doing it. Seeing herself in a video would work better for Tori, Jill thought, but this will have to do for now.

Skating up to Tori after she'd performed the move, Jill said, "So, what do you think?"

"I think you looked awful," Tori replied. "You'd better work on your own double axel before you try to coach someone else."

Jill smiled. "I wasn't doing *my* double axel. I was doing *yours.*"

Tori's mouth dropped open.

"As you yourself just said, Tori, it was awful!"

"You're making fun of me!" Tori cried, her face turning a deep shade of red. "You may think you're the best skater here, like you told Ryan. But that doesn't give you the right to make fun of me!"

"Look, Tori," Jill began. "You're never going to get better if you can't take a little criticism. At the Academy we get raked over the coals every Friday night. Ludmila Petrova and Simon Wells make videos of us skating during the week. Most of the time we don't even know we're being filmed either. They show the videos and critique us—in front of everyone! It can be brutal. You wouldn't last a minute."

"I don't believe Ludmila Petrova and Simon Wells make fun of anyone. You're just plain mean, Jill!" Tori declared.

"Hey," Nikki said, skating over. "What's going on, you two?"

"Tori is mad because I tried to help her," Jill said. "She's the one who asked for advice."

"I'm mad because you made fun of me!" Tori countered loudly.

"At the Ice Academy—" Jill began, prepared to tell her story about the Friday-night videos again so that at least Nikki would understand how she had been trying to help Tori.

But Tori cut Jill off. "This isn't the Ice Academy, Jill. It's Silver Blades. We might do things differently, but we like it that way. Don't we, Nikki?"

Nikki shrugged. "I like Silver Blades all right. But I'm not sure what you guys are fighting about."

"Tori is jealous of me just like she's always been," Jill said. "Jealous that I'm at the Ice Academy and jealous that I'm dating a cool guy like Ryan."

"Jealous?" Tori cried. "You've got to be kidding! You're not as cool as you think you are, Jill."

"You probably wish I didn't come home at all," Jill said. "You were the best skater here once I was out of the way. But now that I've shown up, you've been bumped down a notch. Admit it, Tori, you can't handle it. I've learned a lot at the Academy, and I was only trying to help you. You shouldn't have asked for advice if you didn't want to hear it."

"No, Jill, you're wrong. I shouldn't have asked you to my slumber party. You can just forget about coming!" Tori shouted. "As of now, you're uninvited!"

"That's probably the nicest thing you've ever said to me. I wouldn't go to your slumber party if you paid me!" Jill shouted back, and then she skated furiously off the ice.

10

"**W**e really appreciate your baby-sitting for us tonight, honey," Mrs. Wong said as Mr. Wong helped her into her coat Saturday night. "I'm sorry your slumber party got canceled."

"It doesn't matter," Jill said as she picked up Laurie and settled her on her hip. "I didn't really want to go anyway." For once Jill didn't mind having to baby-sit her younger brothers and sisters. This is probably the best way to smooth things over with Mom and Dad, she told herself. Besides, they deserve a night out too.

Jill noted the time on the living room clock. It was seven o'clock. They're probably all starting in on the pizza right about now, she figured, picturing Danielle, Haley, and Nikki with Tori in her kitchen.

"We won't be late," Mr. Wong said as he opened the

front door. "We're having dinner with the Bradfords. Then we're going back to their house to play cards."

"We'll be at Giovanni's," Mrs. Wong added, referring to a local Italian restaurant. "I left the phone numbers for the restaurant and the Bradfords in the den."

Jill smiled. "I know, Mom. You told me already. Twice."

Kristi, Randi, and the twins said good-bye to their parents, who quickly distributed hugs and left before the little ones had time to ask if they could come too.

As soon as the door closed, Randi spoke up. "Can we bake cookies?" she asked. Her dark eyes looked up at Jill eagerly as she assured her older sister, "I know how."

"Okay. We'll all help," Jill said, setting Laurie down. She brushed off her sweatshirt, which, thanks to Laurie, was covered with soda cracker crumbs. Then she followed Randi, Kristi, Michael, Mark, and Laurie to the kitchen. Henry had spent the day at a friend's house and wouldn't be home for another hour.

Kristi didn't waste any time taking charge in the kitchen. "We need butter," she said, pointing at Mark. He nodded and ran to the refrigerator. "And a big bowl," she added, this time pointing at Michael. "Get the one Dad always uses. The white one in the cupboard next to the sink." The other twin scrambled to follow Kristi's orders.

"I'll get the chocolate chips," Randi declared. But when she started climbing up on the kitchen counter, Jill stopped her.

"Remember what Mom told you," Jill said as she helped Randi back to the floor. "No climbing on the kitchen counters. I'll get the chocolate chips." Jill looked for them, but she found there weren't any in the cupboard where Mrs. Wong usually kept them.

"Oh, no," Randi groaned dramatically when Jill said they were out of chips. "Now we can't make cookies."

"Dad must have used them all up last week when he made cookies for your party, Jill," Kristi said, twisting a strand of her short black hair around her finger. "I guess someone will have to go to the store and get some."

Jill's first thought was to run up to the corner store by herself. And she would have if Henry had been home to watch the kids for a minute. But she couldn't leave Kristi with everyone. She might seem older than eight, but she was still too young to be responsible for the younger ones.

"Everybody get a jacket," Jill said. "Randi, you get Laurie's jacket. We'll walk up to the Minute Mart. I'm sure they have chocolate chips."

Jill had forgotten how long it took to get so many kids ready to go out. But finally everyone had on a jacket and a pair of shoes. She left Henry a note telling him they'd all run out to the store, in case he came home while they were gone. Then she picked up Laurie and joined the other kids outside.

"Want me to get Laurie's stroller?" Kristi asked Jill. "It's in the garage."

"The Minute Mart is pretty close," Jill decided. "She can walk."

Laurie's tiny baby steps made the trip slow going, but then she asked to be carried halfway down the block. At the corner store Jill picked up the chocolate chips while Kristi waited outside with the twins. Jill knew better than to let them come inside, where all sorts of gum, candy, and toys would tempt them. She promised them she'd buy them a pack of gum if they waited for her outside.

When the group arrived home, they discovered Henry in the kitchen. He hummed as he mixed together the cookie ingredients in the bowl on the counter.

"I turned the oven on too," he said. "After I read your note, I got this major craving for chocolate chip cookies, so I started on the dough."

Only Randi seemed disappointed that the cookies were almost made.

"You can stir in the chips," Jill told her eager six-year-old sister. "And spoon the first batch onto the cookie sheet too." Jill opened the bag of chips and dumped it into the bowl. Henry handed Randi the wooden spoon he'd been using.

"You got some phone calls, Jill," Henry said as he dipped a spoon into the raw dough and took a taste.

Randi saw what her brother was doing and sampled the dough too.

"Hey," Jill said. "Easy on that dough. You're supposed to cook it first. Who did you say called?" Jill couldn't resist taking a fingerful of the dough herself.

"One was from Danielle. She said something about being at Tori's all night. Anyway, you're supposed to call her there."

Danielle, Jill thought, I wonder what she wants. I'll have to call her back, but what if I get Tori on the phone? What will I say to her? What will Tori say to me? Jill wasn't even sure how the fight with Tori had started. Maybe I did get a little carried away when I imitated Tori's double axel, Jill thought, but Tori didn't have to go ballistic.

"Who else called?" Jill asked.

"Some guy. I asked for his name but he wouldn't give it," Henry said. "He said he'd call back."

Ryan! Jill thought. It must have been Ryan who called, and I missed it! She glared at the cookie dough, suddenly hating chocolate chip cookies.

She wanted to call Ryan back but she decided against it. And because she dreaded calling Tori's house, she decided to wait awhile and see if Danielle called again.

"I'm going to give Laurie a bath," Jill said. "You guys finish baking the cookies. Henry, you're in charge."

"What about me?" Kristi protested.

"You're second in command," Jill told her. "You can make sure the cookies don't get burned."

Upstairs, Jill turned on the bathwater and waited until it was just the right temperature before plugging up the tub. She'd just put Laurie in the water when Henry called up from the bottom of the stairs.

"Phone!" he said. "It's that guy who called before."

Ryan! Jill looked at Laurie, who was splashing water and playing with a rubber duck. She couldn't leave her alone in the bath, but she really wanted to talk to Ryan. For a moment Jill considered pulling Laurie out of the bath, wrapping her quickly in a towel, and running to answer the phone with her sister in her arms. But Laurie would be upset. She might even cry, and Jill couldn't talk on the phone while Laurie was in her arms crying.

"Tell him to call back in fifteen minutes," Jill shouted reluctantly. Then she bathed her sister and rinsed her off. She cut the bath a little short, but Laurie didn't seem to notice. After drying her off and putting her in a fresh diaper and pajamas, Jill carried Laurie downstairs for one of the cookies.

As Jill was pouring everyone a glass of milk, the phone rang.

"I'll get it," Jill said, springing to her feet. She hurried out of the kitchen and into the den. This has to be Ryan calling back, she said to herself. It has to be.

"Hello?" Jill said breathlessly as soon as she'd picked up.

"Hi, Jill. It's Danielle."

"Oh, hi," Jill said, her voice giving away how disappointed she was.

"Is this a bad time to call?" Danielle asked. "You don't sound very . . . well . . . you know."

"Oh, no," Jill said. "It's okay. It's just that I'm expecting Ryan to call, and I've got to watch the kids and everything."

"Well, I won't keep you long," Danielle said. "I just wanted to call and say we all miss you. Haley and Nikki and Tori are making popcorn and we rented a video. Maybe you could come over to Tori's later, when your parents get home?"

Jill was silent for a moment. She didn't know quite what to say. She didn't want to continue the silly argument she'd had with Tori, but at the same time Tori had told her she didn't want her to go to the slumber party.

"Jill?" Danielle asked. "You still there?"

"I'm still here," Jill said. "It's just that Tori was really angry today at the rink, and I'm not exactly looking forward to going through that again with her, you know? I mean, she asked me for advice, so I gave it to her. And I thought the best way to help her would be to show her exactly what she was doing wrong. Maybe it was too much for her, but at the Academy—"

"But this isn't the Academy," Danielle cut in. "We're in Silver Blades. And we like it. Maybe if you could show us what you've learned without being so, I don't know . . ."

"So what?" Jill said. "Do you think I was being too bossy? Or too tough on her? That's the way it's done at the Academy, and I thought you would want to know what serious training is all about."

"Jill," Danielle said in a tense voice. "We *know* what serious training is. What do you think we've been doing all these years?"

"I'm sorry," Jill said. "I know you all work hard. I

didn't mean that. It's just that they work you twice as hard at the Academy."

"So you keep telling us," Danielle said. "All you ever talk about is the Academy! So are you going to come to Tori's later or not?"

Just then a high-pitched beep sounded in Jill's ear. "Oh, that's my call waiting," Jill said. "Can you hold on a second?"

"Sure," Danielle said.

Jill pressed the button to put the other caller on the line and said, "Hello?"

"Is that you, Jill?" a boy's voice asked.

"Ryan!" Jill said. "I'm glad I finally get to talk to you!"

"So am I," Ryan said. "Listen, I've got a great idea."

"What?" Jill asked eagerly.

"Come rock climbing with Nate and Cindy and me tomorrow. We'll double-date again. We'll go to my favorite place in the mountains, about two hours from here. Nate said he can drive, and it'll be awesome. Think you can come?"

Jill's mind raced. Rock climbing? What would she tell her parents?

"I'd really like to go . . . ," she said. "It's just that, you know, my parents." She felt so babyish even bringing them up.

"Maybe you should let them meet me," Ryan suggested. "I mean, I'm just a regular guy. I'm not the swamp creature or anything. I'll even comb my hair and wear my best jeans."

Jill giggled. How could she pass up spending the day with him tomorrow? He was so much fun. She decided she'd tell her parents she had reserved some extra time on the ice and would be gone most of the afternoon.

"Meet me at the ice rink tomorrow morning," Jill said. "I'll tell my parents I'm skating."

"Great!" Ryan said. "We'll be there at nine-thirty."

Jill was grinning from ear to ear when she hung up. She was so happy, she felt as if she were floating through the house. She didn't think her parents would suspect anything if she was gone most of the day, and she'd be sure she made it home for dinner—Sunday dinner was always a big meal at the Wong house.

In the kitchen she found her sisters and brothers still eating chocolate chip cookies. Henry was taking the last batch out of the oven, and the twins and Laurie were wearing milk mustaches. Jill told Mike and Mark to get washed and ready for bed. Then she wiped Laurie's face and carried her up to her room.

When she'd finally tucked the younger kids into bed, Jill went into her room to decide what to wear for her date tomorrow. Luckily Kristi was downstairs watching TV, so Jill didn't have to explain what she was doing.

Jill tried on several tops, wishing she'd brought more clothes home in her suitcase. Kristi came up and climbed into bed around ten, and Jill went into the bathroom to wash her hair.

She'd just finished blow-drying her hair when she

heard the front door open. Her parents had arrived home later than usual. Jill glanced at her watch and saw that it was a quarter to eleven.

Too late to go to Tori's now, even if I wanted to, Jill thought. Then, with a jolt, she realized she'd forgotten all about someone.

"Oh, no!" Jill said out loud.

She stared at herself in the mirror and shook her head. She'd forgotten to get Danielle back on the line. And that was hours ago.

It's too late to call now, Jill decided. Tori's mother wouldn't appreciate a phone call this late at night. What's Danielle going to think? And Tori? Now *both* of them will be mad at me!

First thing on Sunday morning Jill called Danielle at Tori's house, just before she was about to leave for the rink to meet Ryan. No one answered, so she left a message on the answering machine for Danielle to call her back.

Ten minutes later, as she was leaving for the rink with her father, the phone rang. Jill grabbed the receiver and heard Haley on the other end.

"Did Danielle get the message?" Jill asked anxiously. "I feel so bad. I forgot she was holding on the other line last night. I hope she's not mad at me."

"Well, umm, actually," Haley said, "they all went out to breakfast with Tori's mom. My parents made me come home early so we could go over to my grandmother's. I thought I'd call you to see what happened."

Jill explained that she had been so excited about going rock climbing with Ryan that she'd forgotten all about Danielle. "I remembered around eleven o'clock, but by then it was too late to—"

"You're going *rock climbing*?" Haley interrupted.

"That's right," Jill said. "I really should get going. Ryan's going to meet me at the rink at nine-thirty."

"Jill, you must be losing it," Haley said. "You know you shouldn't be taking risks like that."

"What do you mean?" Jill asked. "We're just going to climb up a mountain. Ryan knows what he's doing."

"I really don't think you should do that," Haley said. "Kathy always told us we had to make priorities, and that we shouldn't do anything that could ruin our skating careers. I mean, you wouldn't go skiing. And hiking is just as risky. What do your parents have to say about it?"

"I'm not telling them," Jill said, rolling her eyes. "It's just a little hike. They don't have to know about it."

"I don't think you should go," Haley said again.

"Well, I don't care what you think," Jill replied. "I've heard enough from everybody telling me what I should and shouldn't do. I'm on vacation, remember? And I want to have some fun."

"Whatever," Haley replied.

Jill said good-bye without giving Haley a message for Danielle. Oh, well, she said to herself. I'll call Danielle when I get home tonight and apologize.

Mr. Wong dropped her off at the rink at nine-thirty. Jill was glad to see that no one she knew was in the locker room when she got there. She didn't have time for a major discussion with Danielle or Tori about what had happened yesterday. Plus, she didn't want them to see her getting ready to go hiking with Ryan.

She quickly brushed her hair and glanced at herself in the mirror. She wore jeans and a Silver Blades sweatshirt. "Well, I guess I'm as ready as I'll ever be," she said, and rushed out of the locker room.

Just as Ryan had promised, Nate's blue VW bug was waiting for them in front of the Ice Arena. Jill hurried over to the car and got in.

"Hi, everybody," Jill said.

"Hi, yourself," Ryan said, putting his arm around her.

"Hey, Jill," Cindy said with a yawn. "Can you believe it's only nine-thirty, and we're going rock climbing?"

Jill laughed. "Actually, since I get up around five almost every morning, this feels really late."

"Amazing!" Cindy exclaimed. "I could never drag myself out of bed as early as you do."

"I'm used to it," Jill said as Nate drove off. "I do it every day but Sunday."

"Even when you're on vacation?" Cindy demanded.

"Yeah," Jill said. "But today I'm really psyched to go hiking." She felt a pang of guilt for lying to her parents about where she was going. But then she glanced over at Ryan and told herself she was doing the right thing. In six days she'd be heading back to Denver. She didn't know when she'd see Ryan again.

"Okay," Nate said as he turned onto the highway headed north, "where exactly are we going?"

"Have you got a map?" Ryan asked, leaning forward.

"It's in the glove compartment." Nate gestured with his hand and Cindy got out the map. She turned around and handed it to Ryan.

"Is that your old skating club sweatshirt?" Cindy asked, fixing her blue eyes on Jill's sweatshirt. Touching the front of her sweatshirt, Jill thought sadly of the day her friends at Silver Blades had given it to her. How had everything grown so complicated between them?

"My friends from Silver Blades gave me this," Jill said. Then she complimented Cindy on her sweatshirt, which had a picture of a rock band on the front.

Cindy laughed. "This is Nate's."

"Okay," Ryan said. He had the map open now and pointed to a big green rectangle. "This is the state park. You stay on this highway most of the trip, Nate. We should see signs when we get close."

"You're the navigator," Nate said. "Don't get us lost."

"Don't worry," Ryan said confidently. He smiled at Jill. "We're going to take a great trail."

"Ryan's not at all afraid of heights," Cindy said. "But some of us are."

"Is this trail dangerous?" Jill asked.

"It's nothing you can't handle," Ryan assured her. "Remember, Jill, I've seen you do amazing things on skates. Rock climbing is going to be a piece of cake for you."

Cindy turned on the radio. The next song that came on was one of Jill's favorites. When Cindy started singing, Jill joined in. Ryan rapped out the beat on the back of the front seat, and Nate drummed the steering wheel.

When they finally reached the state park, it was after eleven. Nate parked and everyone piled out. Then Nate opened the trunk and Ryan pulled out two medium-size backpacks, which held their picnic lunch and other supplies. Ryan and Nate each put on one of the backpacks.

Jill took a deep breath. The air was fragrant with the scent of pine. The sky was cloudless and a brilliant blue. All Jill's doubts faded. This is going to be great! she told herself. No matter what Haley says.

Ryan led the way to the head of one of the trails that started in the parking lot. Jill saw the mountains in the distance and smiled. It reminded her of Denver.

With Ryan still in the lead, they started up the trail. It was a steep uphill path, but Jill felt confident she could handle it. The woods closed around them, and half an hour later Jill said, "It's beautiful here!"

"Yeah, beautiful. But doesn't this trail ever go downhill?" Cindy asked.

Looking over her shoulder, Jill saw that Cindy was flushed and out of breath. Jill felt sorry for her. But she also felt good that she could keep up with an experienced hiker like Ryan without losing her breath. This is a nice workout for me, she decided. It'll keep me in shape.

"Cindy's slowing up, Ryan," Jill reported a little while later. "Maybe we should rest a minute."

"Are you tired?" he asked Jill.

"No, but . . . ," Jill began.

"The trail levels out in a minute. Cindy will feel better," he told Jill. Then he yelled, "Hang in there, Cindy!"

"This is so beautiful," Jill said again, and Ryan said something back that Jill couldn't hear. She wished the trail were a little wider so they could walk side by side.

A moment later the path leveled out just as Ryan had promised. He stopped and turned around. Nate passed Cindy and Jill and stepped up in front of Ryan.

"I think this is too much for Cindy," Nate said.

"I heard that," Cindy said with a breathless laugh. She sat down on a nearby rock. "Just give me a minute and I'll be all right. It is pretty up here."

"Do you want to sit down too, Jill?" Ryan asked.

Jill shook her head. She felt great!

After a few minutes Cindy stood up. "I'm ready to go," she said. "I just wish there weren't all these gnarly roots along the trail to step over. This flat part would be a lot easier to hike if it were really flat."

"You do have to be careful you don't trip on anything," Ryan warned.

"Why not jump over the roots!" Jill suggested.

"Jump over them? We're not all professional athletes," Nate teased.

"What do you mean, jump over them?" Ryan asked with a grin.

"Okay," Jill said boldly. "Step aside and I'll show you

all how to jump." Taking the lead, Jill began leaping over the exposed roots. She held her arms out as if they were wings. Jill felt so exhilarated that she thought she might just soar right off the mountain like an eagle.

She pushed away the warning Haley had given her that morning. I know what I'm doing, she told herself. And I'm tired of everyone else telling me what to do. Haley, my parents, Tori, everybody. I'm old enough to take care of myself. And I'm free! She took another leap, which took her several feet downhill, and landed as if she had springs on her feet.

"No fair," Cindy yelled after her. "You're showing off!"

But instead of making Jill slow down, Cindy's comment egged her on. Jill felt as if she could keep up her current pace indefinitely. Maybe even until the end of the trail!

"Go, Jill!" Ryan yelled. Then Jill heard him say, "Isn't she great?" Jill thought she might explode with happiness.

She kept up her leaping until she reached the end of the ridge. Then she stopped to wait for the others to catch up with her.

"Should we stop and have our picnic here at the top of the hill?" Ryan asked. "It's about twelve-thirty," he added, glancing at his wristwatch. "Or would you rather wait until we get to the springs down in that valley?"

"I could eat now," Nate said, patting his stomach.

Cindy gave him a playful shove. "You're always hungry. I think we should wait. I'd like to find a place that's flatter."

"Jill?" Ryan asked. "How about you?"

Jill looked down the hill. "Let's go a little farther."

Ryan shrugged. "Okay. But going around these boulders is going to take longer than you think."

"Why go around them?" Jill said boldly. Then she scrambled up on the nearest rock. "Why not go down them? We could jump from rock to rock!"

Ryan frowned and shook his head. "I don't know," he said doubtfully. "I've never done that. I don't even know if it's possible."

"Just watch me!" Jill leapt to a boulder that was a few feet away and slightly lower than the one she was on. A perfect landing! she told herself.

"Go, Jill!" Ryan yelled.

Encouraged, Jill jumped again, but this time she spun around in the air one full rotation, as if she were on skates. She did it two more times, picking up speed with each jump.

"She's crazy!" Cindy shouted.

"She's unbelievable," Nate added.

Ryan clapped and whistled. "Way to go, Jill!" he yelled.

Jill felt as if she were giving the performance of her life on ice. She landed again and decided to try a double axel. I wish Tori could see me now, she thought. And Haley too. Pushing off, she twisted twice, gaining enough height, and felt herself whiz through the blue sky. Then she prepared for a perfect landing.

She looked down. With a shock she realized there was no large boulder below to land on. Instead, there was a group of smaller, jagged rocks. She tried to twist away from the sharp rocks, frantically searching for a solid place to land. But there was no smooth surface anywhere!

She came down hard on her left foot. Her ankle bent sharply, and she cried out in pain.

"Jill!" she faintly heard Ryan call.

Jill tried to yell back. She opened her mouth but didn't have the strength to shout. The deep, sharp throbbing in her foot had taken her breath away, and the only sound that came out was a cry of pain.

12

"**J**ill!" she heard Ryan call again. Jill tried to move, but the pain was too terrible. It shot through her foot like a hot, sharp knife, and she gritted her teeth. Her whole foot throbbed. Looking down, she saw that it had started to swell.

"Don't move, Jill," Ryan said, his voice sounding closer. "I'm coming. Don't move."

Jill had never felt so much pain. She felt helpless and frustrated and furious with herself all at once. "How could I do something so stupid?" she murmured. She saw Ryan coming toward her and fought back tears.

"Jill," Ryan said when he finally reached her. "Are you all right?" Jill shook her head. She felt a tear run down her cheek and brushed it away. Then Cindy and Nate were there too.

"Look. We'd better not move her," Ryan said, taking charge. "You two go back and find a ranger. I'll stay here with Jill."

Nate nodded, and he and Cindy turned and started scrambling back up the drop.

"I'm sorry," Jill finally managed to say.

"Forget it," Ryan said. "You just made a mistake." He put his arm around her. "How does it feel?"

"I think I broke something," Jill said. "It's starting to swell."

"Nate and Cindy will be back with help in a few minutes," Ryan assured her. "We'll get you out of here. Then we'll take you to the nearest emergency room."

"My parents . . . ," Jill wailed.

"We'll call them," Ryan said.

"No!" Jill said. "We can't! I'm not supposed to be here."

"We have to call them," Ryan said. "Sooner or later they have to find out."

Jill closed her eyes. It was all too terrible. She remembered what Haley had told her about taking risks. About not blowing her skating career. And I didn't listen, Jill said to herself. Her stomach churned, not so much from the pain, but from fear. When would she be able to skate again?

The next thing she knew, two park rangers were hovering over her. They placed a stretcher on the ground and laid her on it.

"Relax as much as you can," one of the rangers said.

"We'll get you out of here safely. The ambulance will be waiting in the parking lot by the time we get there."

Jill squeezed her eyes shut, trying to stop the tears as the men strapped her securely to the stretcher. She didn't know which would be worse: facing her parents and telling them she'd lied, or finding out that she'd ruined her future as a skater.

"Your parents are on their way," Ryan said as he stepped in front of the curtain separating Jill from the other patients in the emergency room.

"Did you call them?" Jill asked. The nurse had cut the leg off her jeans, and she now had a splint on her left ankle. According to the doctor on duty, Jill's foot was definitely broken. But she couldn't have a permanent cast until the swelling went down.

Ryan shook his head. "The nurse at the desk called them."

Jill nodded. She didn't feel very brave, but she didn't want Ryan and the others to know how scared she was. "You can all go if you want."

"That's okay, Jill. I'll stay," Ryan said. "Unless you want me to go, that is."

Jill closed her eyes and shook her head. "I don't want you to go," she said. Ryan moved closer to her and sat down. He took her hand in his.

"We'll all stay," Nate said. He put his arm around

Cindy, who shook her head. "This is just awful, Jill. I'm really sorry. Have the painkillers started working?"

Jill nodded. The doctor had given her pills to relieve the throbbing pain, but her fear was still intense.

In a much shorter time than Jill would have liked, Mr. and Mrs. Wong arrived. With one quick glance at them, Jill could tell that they were angry and confused.

"Jill!" Mrs. Wong said, hurrying to Jill's side. "What happened? What are you doing here?"

"And who are these people?" Mr. Wong added, scowling at Ryan, Cindy, and Nate.

"They're my friends," Jill said. "This is Ryan McKensey. He's sort of our neighbor."

"McKensey?" Mr. Wong repeated, his scowl deepening. "What is going on? Aren't you supposed to be skating right now, Jill?" He studied Jill's foot for a moment, then her face. "How did you get here? I dropped you off at the Arena this morning, and now you're two hours away from Seneca Hills." Mr. Wong's voice was getting louder as he spoke.

"We better go," Ryan said softly. "Good-bye, Jill. I'll call." With that, the threesome fled. Jill watched Ryan disappear behind the curtain and knew she'd have to face her parents now and tell the truth.

"Jill, explain yourself," Mr. Wong demanded. "Where have you been?"

"I lied," Jill confessed. "And this isn't the first time

either. I've been lying all along." She took a shaky breath. "I'm really sorry."

Mr. and Mrs. Wong didn't say anything. Jill could tell that they were in shock. Her father looked angry. And her mother looked hurt and confused. Fresh tears started to flow down Jill's cheeks. She wiped them away and began to explain everything—Ryan, the hike, missing her skating practice—an entire week's worth of lies.

"I thought you might not let me go out with Ryan," Jill said. "Because he's in high school. It all seems so stupid and immature now. I wanted to be on my own during this vacation. I felt like I'd grown up while I was at the Academy, but . . . I guess I was wrong." Jill wished she could go back in time. She wished she had told her parents about Ryan, even if they'd said she couldn't date him. Then none of this would have happened, and she would have been at the Ice Arena today instead of showing off like an idiot.

"You should have been honest with us, Jill," Mrs. Wong said. "We've always trusted you. You gave us no reason not to. And now this. I just don't understand," she said, looking with a searching expression into Jill's eyes. "Why?"

"I wish I had told you the truth. I really do," Jill said, staring down at her foot. "Once I started lying, I couldn't stop. It was horrible."

"But none of this explains what's happened," Mrs. Wong said. "You're hurt, Jill. Badly, it seems."

"We were hiking," Jill said. "And I started acting like a jerk, jumping on the rocks—"

But before she could go on with her story, Mr. Wong held up his hands. "What about your skating?" he interrupted.

"I didn't go skating this morning," Jill said. "Ryan picked me up at the Arena—"

"I mean, how will you skate with this injury?" Mr. Wong asked.

"I don't know," Jill whispered as more hot tears streamed down her face. "I don't know."

On Monday afternoon Jill's parents brought her to the orthopedist, who looked over the X rays of her foot. Jill had a compound fracture and torn ligaments. The cast, which had been put on the night before at the emergency room, would have to stay on for six to eight weeks. After that she'd have many more weeks of physical therapy.

When Jill asked Dr. Alison Springer when she'd be able to skate again, the doctor said she couldn't give her a definite answer. "We'll have to see how the bones heal, and how well therapy goes. I can't make a prognosis at this point. But I can tell you that you'll have to stay off the foot for two months, and then therapy will be another one to two months."

"But what can I do to make it heal faster?" Jill said. She explained that she was training to compete in the

Olympics and that she had to get back on the ice as soon as possible.

"The best thing you can do now," Dr. Springer said, "is keep the foot elevated and get lots of rest. Whatever you do, stay off that foot."

"Jill's home!" Michael announced later in the afternoon as Jill clumped into the house on her crutches.

"Can I sign your cast now?" Mark asked eagerly.

"Stay out of your sister's way," Mrs. Wong said to the twins.

Jill kept moving until she reached the den. She collapsed onto the couch. Then she propped her foot up on three pillows. Her parents followed her into the room and sat down in two chairs, facing the couch.

Jill looked at her parents and knew she needed to apologize to them again.

"I know I might have totally blown my skating career," she began. "It's bad enough that I'll lose months of practice, and I'll be terribly out of shape once this heals. But that's not the worst of it."

She tried to calm herself. I have to face this like an adult, she told herself. I have to take full responsibility. And I'm *not* going to cry.

"The worst of it is that I've let you both down. You've made big sacrifices. I know it hasn't been easy. Dad, you've had to work overtime for my skating. And, Mom,

I know you went right back to work after Laurie was born because we needed the money. And you've had to arrange your days around my schedule, driving me to and from the Arena every day."

Her parents sat silently, gazing at her with disappointment. Her father still seemed angry, and her mother looked very tired. Jill fought back the tears that were rising again.

"I want you to know how sorry I am," she said. "And I'll try to make it up to you." She looked down at the floor. "I'm really sorry."

"I know you are," said Mrs. Wong. "Your father and I still don't see how you could have done this. But we all need to move on from here."

Jill couldn't believe her parents weren't yelling at her. They weren't telling her how stupid she'd been. But their silence on the subject spoke more loudly than words.

"Don't you think you should tell the people at the Academy that you're not coming back?" Mr. Wong asked.

Jill closed her eyes for a moment and nodded.

"Ludmila Petrova is expecting you back in Denver on Saturday."

Jill knew there was no way to avoid it—she'd have to call Ludmila and tell her everything. And there was no point in waiting any longer.

"I'll call now," Jill said. "Would you hand me the phone, Dad?"

With the phone in her lap, Jill slowly dialed the number and asked for the Academy's co-owner. It was one of the hardest things she'd ever had to do.

"I have bad news," Jill said slowly when Ludmila got on the line. "Really bad news."

"What is it?" Ludmila asked, concerned.

"I'm not coming back," Jill blurted out. She stared at her parents' long faces and swallowed tears. "I mean I won't be back Saturday. Maybe not ever."

"Slow down, Jill," Ludmila replied. "I don't understand what you're talking about."

"Um—I've injured my foot. I mean, I broke it." Jill explained the accident in a shaky voice. "I'm in a cast, and I won't be able to skate. For months," she finished.

Jill waited for Ludmila's reply. But there was silence on the other end. Then she heard a sigh, and Ludmila said, "I see."

"I'm sorry I won't be coming back," Jill said, wishing Ludmila would yell at her, tell her how foolish she'd been—something.

"I'm sorry too, Jill," Ludmila replied quietly. "You had a lot of potential."

"I'll miss you. All of you," Jill said as tears rolled down her face.

Ludmila asked to speak with Mr. and Mrs. Wong. After talking over the medical details with them, Ludmila told Jill to call again in several weeks. And that was all. She hadn't said she'd save Jill's room for her.

Or that she'd tell her coach or Bronya what had happened.

Jill said good-bye but held on to the phone receiver for a moment after Ludmila hung up. So much had changed so quickly. Her whole future as a champion skater had disappeared in one split second.

13

"That's the doorbell," Jill told Kristi on Monday. She had just started to write a letter to Bronya explaining why she wouldn't be back. Kristi had been keeping her company while Mr. Wong and Henry were at a baseball game and Mrs. Wong was at the park with the younger kids.

"I'll see who it is," Kristi said as she stood up. She nodded at the TV set. "Can I freeze the video?"

"Sure," Jill agreed. They were watching one of Kristi's favorite movies, about a girl who wanted her own horse. Jill was having trouble concentrating on the action, but Kristi thought it was the best movie ever made.

Jill wondered who was at the door. She doubted it was Ryan—he probably wouldn't be too eager to see her parents for a while. He had said he'd call, but so far he hadn't. She had left a message, but there was still no word. Ryan was probably afraid her parents would tell him not to call anymore—or at least she hoped that was it.

Jill sighed and bent her leg at the knee a few times. It was getting stiff from being propped up in the same position.

"You've got a visitor," Kristi said excitedly as she hurried back into the den.

Then, before Jill could even ask Kristi who it was, Ryan came into the den too.

"Ryan!" Jill cried. "It's so good to see you. I was just thinking about you."

"I guess I can't watch the rest of my video right now, huh?" Kristi asked, and Jill shook her head.

"It'd be really nice if you found something else to do," Jill told Kristi. "In another room."

"I'll be in the kitchen," Kristi said.

"Nice kid," Ryan said.

"Kristi's great," Jill said. "A couple of months ago she thought she was getting my old room all to herself for good. Now it looks like I'm back for a while. She hasn't complained once either."

"It's that bad, huh?" asked Ryan. "You're really not going back to Denver?"

"Not now. Maybe not ever." Jill took a deep breath, holding back the tears. She couldn't believe she might never skate at the Academy again. "The doctor I saw today said we'd have to wait about two months to see how my foot is healing. He said we'd know then whether or not I'll need surgery."

"Too bad," Ryan said, shaking his head. "I'm really sorry. I feel like this whole thing is my fault. I never should have talked you into going hiking."

"It's not your fault, Ryan. It's mine. I was showing off," Jill said.

"I wasn't sure if I should come over," Ryan said. "Your parents seemed really upset at the hospital. I didn't think I'd be very welcome. But I saw your mother and the kids at the park a few minutes ago and she told me to visit you. She's really nice."

"I know," Jill said. She knew she was fortunate to have parents who had been so supportive of her skating all these years.

"So, what are you going to do now that you're stuck here in Seneca Hills?" Ryan asked, and Jill thought about her friends again. She hadn't told any of them about her accident. She wondered if Danielle was still mad at her. And if Tori would ever want to speak to her again after their argument. It seemed as if it all had happened so long ago. She didn't want to fight with them anymore.

The doorbell rang again, interrupting her thoughts.

"I'll get it!" Kristi yelled from the kitchen.

Jill heard a commotion in the front hall. A moment later Kristi appeared at the doorway with Tori, Nikki, Danielle, and Haley. They all stared at Jill's foot, and for a while no one said a word.

"I didn't expect to see you guys," Jill finally said. Then she quickly added, "But I'm really glad you're here. Really glad. Come in. Sit down."

"Kathy told us about your accident. Your dad called her," Danielle said. "What happened?"

The four girls still hadn't moved from their position at the doorway.

"Uh, did we come at a bad time?" Haley asked, nodding meaningfully at Ryan.

"Oh, no," said Ryan. He stood up. "I'd better go. I left my dog tied up outside, and I shouldn't leave him that way too long."

"You can bring Groucho in if you want," Jill said.

"No, that's okay," Ryan said. "But I'll be back—I mean, now that I know it's okay. I'll call tomorrow, Jill."

Jill nodded. "You know where to find me," she said.

When Ryan left, the Silver Blades gang made themselves at home.

"How bad is it?" Tori asked nervously as she took a seat.

"Bad," Jill said. "Compound fracture and torn ligaments," she added. "Six to eight weeks in a cast, and then more time in physical therapy."

Jill looked at her friends' concerned faces. She knew she had a lot of explaining to do. First about the accident, and then about how she had treated them.

"I brought this on myself," she began to explain, looking at Haley. "I thought I knew my limits. And I didn't want anyone telling me what to do." A picture of herself sailing toward those jagged rocks flashed through her mind, and she shuddered.

"I was showing off on the rocks with Ryan and his friends, and I totally lost control."

"Anyone could have done the same thing," Haley said sympathetically.

Jill shook her head. "No. I was really showing off bad. Just like I did at the rink." Jill looked at Tori. "I know I was kind of mean to you the other day, Tori. I shouldn't have acted like such a know-it-all. I don't know how you guys put up with me."

"Forget about it," Tori said. "We were a little jealous because you'd gotten so good, that's all."

"Yeah, but I went too far," Jill said. "I was totally caught up in being this big star from the Ice Academy. I thought I was some kind of hotshot. And then when Ryan started going out with me, I totally lost it, because he was, like, this older guy." Jill sighed as she stared down at the cast on her foot.

"And I'm really sorry I forgot you were holding on the phone, Dani," she continued.

"Look, we'll understand if you don't want to talk about any of this," Danielle assured her. "Just say the word, Jill, and we'll drop it."

"That's okay. I can talk about it. But first I want to tell you guys how glad I am to see you," Jill said, her eyes filling with tears. "I'm really sorry I've been such a jerk."

"Kathy told us you were probably stressed out from training so hard at the Academy," Tori said. "She said that sometimes training too hard can wind you up to the point where you get sort of frantic."

Jill frowned. "Did you guys really talk to Kathy about me?"

"We had to talk to someone," Danielle said. "We were worried about you, Jill. You just weren't acting like yourself."

"I guess I got carried away," Jill admitted.

"Well, it's over now," Danielle said. "And we're all friends again."

"Right now I can use all the friends I can get. The specialist said that depending on how my ankle heals . . . well, I don't know if I'll ever be able to skate competitively again."

All five girls were silent. The idea of never being able to skate again was just too awful for any of them to think about.

"Does your foot hurt a lot?" Nikki asked.

"It throbs a little if I don't keep it elevated," Jill said.

"We'll help you get on your feet again," Tori said confidently. "In fact," she said, smiling slyly, "now that I've heard what happened, I've decided that what you really need is a lesson from me on how to *fall*. It's one of the first things an ice-skater needs to learn, you know."

Jill chuckled. "I guess I deserved that."

"But seriously, Jill. We'll help you all we can," Nikki promised.

"Thanks, guys." Jill smiled. "Hey, in a few days I'll be back at Grandview Middle School."

"Cool! Danielle and I can help you carry your books

while you hobble around on those crutches," Nikki offered, smiling.

"Some piece of bad luck," Tori said, shaking her head.

"Not all my luck is bad, though. Having you guys for friends is good luck," Jill said, and she meant it. "And I'm going to turn my bad luck around," she added.

Somehow, some way, I'm going to skate again, she vowed silently. I just have to!

She pulled out her pen and waved it in the air. "Hey! Who wants to sign my cast?"

Tori, Nikki, Haley, and Danielle all reached for the pen at once.